LYNNE STEWART

TEMPTING HIS TRUE MATE

BOOK TWO IN THE TRUE MATE SHIFTER SERIES

For the Ellas who worry life is passing them by.
Your time is coming.

Chapter 1

"Now boarding first class for Flagstaff."

The flight attendant beamed at all of us from her podium next to the gate. The plane currently sitting on the tarmac had been delayed for almost four hours, and the humans awaiting takeoff had seemed dangerously close to rioting during the last thirty minutes or so of our wait.

Even with that positive announcement, her chipper tone was wasted on the crowd's grumbling. It didn't seem like she noticed at all.

She cheerfully helped the impeccably groomed businessmen and women wearing designer clothes into the tunnel. I hesitated before joining them, feeling more out of place than ever.

"Just first class, hon." A girl -or woman, rather- with bright blonde highlights looked at my faded knock-off jeans and old tennis shoes from over her sunglasses. When I didn't respond, she gave an annoyed sigh and turned her attention back to her phone.

My cheeks reddened, betraying my embarrassment. My discomfort caused my wolf to growl from her corner in the back of my mind. She didn't understand what the problem was or that the woman was insulting me, but she was completely aware of its effect on my emotions. It was times like this I wished shifting in front of humans wasn't such a big deal. My wolf was much more adept at handling rude people than I was.

In the woman's favor, I didn't exactly look the part of someone who belonged in a first-class seat, but my sister, Mariam, and my soon-to-be brother-in-law, Trace, had insisted on splurging for the upgrade. My curiosity had won out late last night, and a quick Google search told me they had paid more for my round-trip ticket than I made in two weeks working at the Dark Claw Bakery. But hey, if that's how they wanted to spend their money, who was I to judge them?

A seed of guilt planted itself in my stomach at the thought. I had been pretty judgmental about everything to do with them lately, but that came from a place of jealousy. I knew it and could easily own up to it, but nothing could take away the sting of unfairness that surrounded my sister's good fortune.

For one thing, Mariam had done everything wrong. It would be easier to stomach her meeting her true mate and falling in love before me if she had played by the rules, but that's not what had happened. She had broken the moon goddess's rules on werewolf celibacy, ran and hid from her true mate for a month, and then abandoned him again for a weekend in Vegas with her friend, Patrick.

She didn't leave with Patrick. Patrick took her from Tumblewild against her will, my wolf reminded me gently.

I sighed and had to acknowledge the truth in that, but even just considering all the other things, it wasn't fair that

Mariam was now having a mating ceremony with the man of her dreams. Her true mate was everything I had hoped for, and she had been willing to throw it away. Even now, the thought caused my blood to boil.

"Ticket, please," the flight attendant chirped. Her smile reflected none of the other human's judgment about me riding in first class, but she was probably used to way weirder things than an under-dressed passenger.

I let her scan the boarding pass on my phone, and I followed the others to the rows of luxurious leather seats. This was my second time ever flying on an airplane, but it was already infinitely better than the first. Memories of sitting in coach and holding back Mariam's hair as she threw up during takeoff were permanently etched in my mind.

I was surprised that no other members of our pack were on this flight for the mating ceremony. If nothing else, I would have expected her old friends and Jeremy, our alpha, to be somewhere on the plane. Mariam had caused a massive stir in the pack when she had run from Trace, but it had seemed like all had been forgiven when the ceremony announcement was made. Maybe they had opted to drive or were taking a different airline. The ceremony was still three days away. There was time to catch another flight.

Whatever the reason, I was instantly grateful for the airline's complimentary eye cover and the sleeping aid I kept stashed in my purse. If I was going to survive this mating ceremony, I would need to be well-rested, and it wouldn't hurt to get a head start on that before landing.

———

The thud of the plane landing woke me from a deep sleep. The trip from Sacramento to Flagstaff only took about two hours, but apparently, I needed the rest, and the sleeping aid had done the trick. Having the metabolism of a werewolf also meant that there was nothing left to help calm my racing emotions.

On the one hand, it was a relief to see Mariam settle down with a man who would no doubt provide her with the structure she needed. As her mate, Trace would ensure she was disciplined when she was out of line and ensure that she was safe above all else. That alone was a massive weight off my shoulders. Trying to assert some semblance of control over Mariam after our parents died had been a full-time job. I would gladly hand over her care to the alpha of Tumblewild.

But the green-eyed monster lurked just below the surface in my thoughts. Not only was Mariam totally against bonding with a mate until a few months ago, but she was also almost fifteen years younger than me. Seeing her being handed my dreams on a silver platter was hard. It didn't help that Trace reminded me a lot of our dad, either. I had dreamt of having a mate like our father since… well, forever, and now that was becoming a reality for my much, *much* younger sister while I waited on the sidelines. Typical.

I hauled my bag out of the luggage return and rolled it to the arrival area. Mariam had said that their beta would be there to pick me up, giving me only a name (Randy) and a vague description that could fit most male werewolves (tall, sulky, built like a Greek god). Thankfully, he recognized me instantly and came forward out of the crowd.

"Ella Hinder, I presume?" He said it like a question, but he was already taking the suitcase from my hands like he knew the answer.

"You must be Randy." I gave him a small smile, matching the one he offered me. "I hope you weren't waiting long. The flight was delayed for—"

"Almost four hours," he interrupted, shaking his head. "Under normal circumstances, I probably would have left and come back later, but right now, the alpha house is insane, so sticking around here for a long lunch was a nice break."

I groaned inwardly, knowing that I would probably be expected to be very involved with the mating ceremony preparations. *Just relax*, I scolded myself. *One weekend, then this will be over, and everything can go back to normal.*

My wolf huffed her disagreement. Since Mariam had left, my wolf and I had felt so alone in my parents' house by ourselves. Wolves were communal creatures by nature, and although we still had the comforts of being part of the pack, it was hard coming back to an empty home every night.

Randy led me to a large SUV parked in the visitors' lot. When we got in the car, the silence between us felt deafening. "Mariam told me you and your mate live in the alpha house with her and Trace."

I wasn't entirely sure why I said that or how I was hoping he would respond. The lack of conversation just felt too awkward to let it continue indefinitely. But that was just me: always on edge and uncomfortable. My social skills could use some improvement, to say the least.

To my relief, he nodded. "We have a beta apartment on the bottom floor, but we spend a lot of time in their living areas and the home office upstairs. Of course, you'll have a room in the alpha house whenever you visit, too."

I smiled, but my heart sank a little bit. According to Mariam, Randy was happily married to Trace's sister. There's no way he would understand how hard it would be for me to come back and visit, let alone stay in the same house as them. It was like having a front-row seat to everything that was out of my reach. Plus, I wouldn't even be a third wheel with the betas there. I'd be a fifth wheel and even more useless.

Maybe Trace would allow Mariam to visit Dark Claw by herself every once in a while. That was the hope I was going to cling to anyway.

The drive out to the Tumblewild pack was a beautiful one. Large trees and miles of clear sky followed us the entire way. I could easily see why a pack of werewolves would be interested in living in such a place. My wolf was yipping and prancing around like a pup at the thought of running through the dense woods with our sister. I wished I felt even a fraction of her enthusiasm, but instead, I wanted the drive to last forever. We arrived at the alpha house all too soon.

I sucked in a sharp breath as the building came into view. It was massive, confirming the considerable wealth the first-class ticket had hinted at. What kind of pack was Mariam joining anyway? A mafia? Some type of werewolf royalty?

"I'll take your bag up to your room if you want to catch

up with Mariam," Randy offered. "It has an ensuite bath with a tub, too, if you're tired from the flight and need to rest."

I gave him a tentative smile, similar to the one at the airport, to acknowledge the kind gesture. I would absolutely be retreating to my room as soon as possible, but it's not like I could say that out loud. I followed Randy through the front door and into the oversized foyer. The house looked peaceful from the outside but inside was as chaotic as he made it sound. There were people coming and going from all directions, shouting questions and requests to each other over the madness. In the middle of it all was Mariam, with what looked like a plate of random bite-sized desserts. I had to admit that the smell made my mouth water. The air was filled with a sweet cinnamon scent, but much better than anything I had ever smelled working at the bakery back home. Maybe the caterer would be willing to share the recipe so I could recreate it for the wolves living in Dark Claw.

Even from a distance, my sister had a different glow and vibe about her. She had changed a lot over the past month and a half. She had matured, and it was easy to see that she was relaxed. She was a woman in love and secure in her place in the world.

It must be nice.

A smile swept across Mariam's face as our eyes met. She handed the plate to the woman with a clipboard who was trying to get her attention and ran to greet me with a hug.

Our family had never been overly affectionate, and the sudden display caught me off guard. I froze, arms pinned awkwardly at my side. When she didn't let up, I gently moved my hand to pat her on the back.

"I've missed you so much, Ella. I'm so happy you're here," Mariam said, giving me one last squeeze. "Come on. Let me introduce you to Trace."

"We've already met," I quipped. It was true. When Mariam had decided to give her mate the slip, he had searched our house several times over and had insisted on interrogating me himself. Of course, in his haste to find my sister, it is entirely possible that he might not remember very much about those conversations.

"Oh, yeah," she said, having the decency to look at least a little sheepish. "I forgot about that. Well, let's go, and you guys can catch up."

She took me by the hand and gave it a solid tug. I turned to thank Randy, but he was long gone. My suitcase had to be with him, reminding me that he had mentioned something about an ensuite tub in the guest room. I carefully untangled my fingers from her grip. "Actually, Mare, I'm a little tired after the flight. Could I just rest and see you both at dinner tonight?"

A flicker of disappointment dashed across her face, but it was gone as quickly as it came.

"Of course. Sorry! I should have offered you some time to rest after traveling. I'm just so excited you're here, but I'll show you where the guest room is."

"I can manage," I said. "Just tell me which room. You've got a lot going on down here, and I don't want to take you from it."

"Okay, if you're sure," she said. "Up the stairs, third door on the right—"

"Thanks! See you at dinner!"

I scurried away, leaving Mariam standing on her own. Of course, I knew I was being abrupt, but I couldn't wait another minute. I needed time alone to recharge before facing Trace and my sister together.

The first thing I did after finding the guest room was lean against the door and slowly let out the breath I had been unintentionally holding in. I sank to the floor and inhaled more of the same sweet smell that had greeted me when I entered the alpha house.

I frowned. How had the pastry chef managed to infuse every inch of the home with the delicious aroma? Was the HVAC system circulating it from the kitchen all the way upstairs?

My wolf took notice, too. She had been uncharacteristically quiet since we entered the alpha house, and now I could see why. Her nostrils flared, and she had a thousand-yard stare like she was concentrating on the scent and trying to memorize it. Her ears twitched, and her muscles were tense, almost as if she was expecting something to happen at any moment.

The weight of her gaze made me think she could really use some down time, too. I pulled myself to my feet and walked into the oversized bathroom attached to the fancy guest suite. The clawfoot tub had a large assortment of bath bombs and body wash to choose from, but I idly wished I could cleanse myself in the cinnamon that clung to the air.

I shook my head to rid myself of the stupid idea and began stripping off my clothes and running the warm water. I settled into the bath, tilting my head back and closing my eyes as the heat enveloped me completely. The tub back home was nowhere near this deep and luxurious. I knew right then that I would be taking a lot of baths on this trip.

I had almost fallen asleep when pounding on the bedroom door startled me awake. I blinked against the light in the room, confused about the urgency behind the sound.

"Yes? I'm in the bathroom. Is everything okay?" I cringed. Of course, that made it sound like I was answering while sitting on the toilet or something. "I mean… I'm taking a bath. Do you need me, Mariam?"

There was a brief silence and then louder pounding. The knocking turned frantic. I scrambled out of the tub, grabbing a terrycloth robe off its hook, and praying there wasn't a serious emergency. I was almost to the door when it suddenly flew off the hinges and crashed onto the floor at my feet. Trace Everett stood in the hallway, just outside the bedroom's threshold. He was as huge and intimidating as I remembered, but this time he was struggling to restrain another male werewolf with a mop of dark brown hair and eyes that looked almost feral. The other man was much smaller than Trace, almost scrawny in comparison, but he was putting up a decent fight to break free from the alpha's grasp. The smell radiating off him was the same cinnamon I had been enjoying earlier, but now it was much more intense.

His penetrating stare zeroed in on me, and a single word fell from his lips that made me want to go back into the bathroom and hide.

"Mate."

Chapter 2

I cinched the robe tighter around my waist, feeling exposed to the crowd peering into the bedroom from the hallway. The commotion had grabbed not only the attention of Trace but also Mariam and several others from downstairs, who were now looking on with a great deal of curiosity. My brain was doing mental gymnastics, trying to understand what was happening.

My wolf, on the other hand, had no difficulty putting two and two together. She was howling and thumping her tail with excitement, trying desperately to force a shift and face the crazed werewolf herself. At least now, the stranger seemed to be settling a little, though the fire in his eyes was just as bright as before.

"Mate," he rumbled again. "I can't believe you're here." The word sent a shiver down my spine. There was no way this man was my mate. Everything about him was the opposite of what I was hoping for. For years, I had pictured a strong, handsome authoritarian whisking me away from Dark Claw. Basically, the same fairy tale that Mariam had with Trace. But the shifter before me had the build of a poet or maybe that of a college professor, not the linebacker I had conjured up in my dreams. Tall and lean, it was entirely possible that even I weighed more than him, and his clean-shaven baby face left no doubt that he was much younger than me.

The thought made me shutter. I was almost thirty-seven. Mating with a werewolf in his early twenties, or -goddess forbid- his late teens was simply out of the question. The idea alone had the proverbial effect of taking a cold shower, shutting down any argument my wolf might make for how appealing he was.

"I think there's been a mistake," I said as gently as possible. I didn't want to embarrass the young man in front of all these people, the members of his pack that he would have to see every day for the rest of his life. I gave the small crowd in the doorway a pointed look. "Can we have some privacy, please?"

That was enough to free them from their collective trance, and it earned me a few guilty smiles. The group shuffled away, leaving just Mariam and Trace with me and the young man.

He scowled at my words. "There is no mistake. We're mates. *True* mates. Can't you feel it?"

I chewed on the inside of my cheek, not wanting to answer that question or even entertain the idea at all. Sure, I felt drawn to him. The scent surrounding him was exactly what Mariam and everyone had described when meeting their true mate. But the moon goddess had to be confused here. This wasn't romantic. It was horrifying.

"Look," I said. "I don't know who you are or even anything about you. I'm just here for the wedding, and then I'm going back home. I'm telling you, there has been some kind of mix-up."

Mariam stepped forward and cleared her throat. "Gabe, will you be alright if Trace lets you go? You're not going to attack Ella or anything, right?"

The man's -Gabe's- eyes widened, and he became still enough for Trace to release him from the hold he was in. "You're Ella? Mariam's sister?"

I frowned. "You're Gabe?" Mariam had gone on and on about the werewolf named Gabriel, who had helped her when she first came to the Tumblewild pack. She had been on the run and hiding from Trace, only to discover that he was the alpha of the pack she had grown attached to. Gabe had allowed her to live in his spare room and had even gotten her a job when she had arrived in the pack using an assumed name. Using my name as an assumed name, to be exact.

A smile broke out across Gabe's youthful features. "Goddess, I love hearing you say my name. It takes on a whole new meaning coming from your lips."

My cheeks flamed red. He sounded like a kid with a crush. He *was* a kid with a crush, actually. One look at my sister told me that she found the whole thing pretty exciting, a clear contrast to the dread I was feeling.

"Ella, this is perfect! You can stay in Tumblewild, and you won't have to go back home to Dark Claw after the mating ceremony!" She was practically giddy over the idea.

I sighed. "Mariam, believe me. This is a mistake. Gabe is not my true mate. And at the moment, I want nothing more than to put on a pair of pajamas, take a nap, and forget this ever happened."

For a minute, Gabe looked at me like I had kicked his wolf, but then a dangerous glint filled his eyes, and determination set across his face. "Will you two allow me some privacy with Ella? It seems like we have a few things we need to discuss."

Trace hesitated and looked toward Mariam for help on what to do. He had been uncharacteristically quiet for the entire argument. I wondered if the situation reminded him of the first encounter he had with my sister. I hadn't been there to see it for myself, but the gossip around Dark Claw indicated that it hadn't gone very well, either.

"Are you okay with that, Ella?" Mariam asked, looking from me to Gabe and then back to me again.

She was obviously struggling with what to do now that her best friend was looking at me like I was something to eat. *That makes two of us*, I thought.

"It's fine," I lied. It wasn't fine. But maybe if we were alone, he would be more willing to listen to reason. Maybe some of this bravado was him putting on a show to avoid having his ego bruised.

"Okay, then. We'll be just down the hall, so if you need anything, just call for us." She said the last part with a pointed look at Gabe, almost as if it was a warning that they would be able to hear me if I screamed. However unreassuring that was, I was grateful for her attempt to make me feel better.

Gabe nodded, but his eyes remained fixed on me. We stood there staring at each other long after the door had shut, leaving the two of us completely alone in the bedroom.

"Listen, Gabe—"

"You're just so beautiful," he interrupted. He took a step closer and reached up so that his thumb grazed my cheek. "I knew you would be amazing and so worth the wait. I just didn't know you would be… perfect."

I swallowed hard, refusing to acknowledge the butterflies that were fluttering in my lower stomach. "Seriously, Gabe. You couldn't have been waiting that long to find a mate. How old are you? Nineteen?" *Please say no, please say no. Don't be a teenager*, I begged him silently.

He barked a laugh. "I'm hardly a kid, Ella. I'll be twenty-eight in a few months."

The uncomfortable feeling that I was committing a crime by being alone in a room with him dissipated slightly, but twenty-seven was still young. *Too* young.

"You sure about that? Never mind. It doesn't matter. I'm not interested in dating a twenty-seven-year-old, either," I said, cringing at the thought. His age put almost an entire decade of difference between us. When I was a little girl, I used to imagine falling in love with my true mate. But at that time, Gabe wouldn't have even been born yet.

Gabe quirked an eyebrow, his warm brown eyes dancing with humor. "Do you really think a couple of years in age difference matters, Ella? What, when you're eighty, I'll be seventy-nine or something? Age isn't important."

"More like you'll be seventy when I'm eighty," I scoffed, taking a step back to force some distance between us. *Why had Mariam never mentioned how hypnotic his dark eyes were?* "But it doesn't matter. I'm sorry, Gabe, but I'm not attracted to you in that way. And I'm waiting for my true mate. I'm not interested in anything else."

For the first time since barging into my bedroom, Gabe

looked a little unsure of himself.

"Are you really not attracted to me at all, Ella?" His voice was strained, like the question was painful to ask. He reached to brush some strands of wet hair away from my face. His hand strayed lower, tracing my collarbone that the robe had left exposed.

I sucked in a breath at his touch. It lit a fire inside me, and heat pooled between my legs. And it was at that moment, before I could try to hide it, that he saw everything. He saw my desire, and he knew the effect he could have on me. He knew how weak I was to temptation, and his look of concern shifted until he appeared almost predatory.

He quickly closed the distance between us, forcing my chin up so that my eyes met his. I swallowed hard again.

"What are you doing?" I asked, hoarse and shaky. I licked my lips nervously, which only drew his attention to them.

"I think you know exactly what I'm doing," he purred. "Isn't it what you want, Ella? I'll savor the taste of you. I'll make you feel so good, like the goddess you are."

I shivered at his words, my brain fogging over. I was about to give in, to reach up and draw his mouth down to mine, but there was a hesitant knock at the door that severed the connection between us. I stumbled backward, shaking my head to clear my mind from the spell he had put me under. Gabe growled, irritated at the interruption.

"Is everything alright?" Mariam's voice was a little muffled through the solid wood, but it was enough for me to recognize her concerned tone. I slipped past Gabe and opened the door before he could stop me. I could tell that my eagerness to let her in annoyed him even more.

"Hey, yeah, I… I mean, *we* were just coming out. I mean, Gabe was actually leaving. I still need to get dressed, as you can see. Ha-ha." Mariam's eyes widened at my disheveled rambling, and even I had to admit that my fake laugh at the end was a little excessive. There was no way I wanted to analyze how close I had been to sucking Gabe's face off, and being overly cheerful and perky apparently helped prevent me from focusing on that.

"Good talk, Gabe. Glad we could get that sorted out." I opened the door wider and sharply gestured for him to leave. For one horrible moment, I thought he was going to refuse, and I would be stuck wearing the bathrobe for the rest of eternity, but instead, he flashed me a knowing smile and moved to walk out the door without putting up a fight.

"I agree, Ella. I'm glad we were able to clear all this up." I let out a slow breath and tried to close the door behind him, but he caught it at the last minute. "I look forward to seeing you at dinner tonight, mate. In fact, I think we should go out to celebrate. I'll tell everyone not to expect us this evening."

I shut the door hastily as soon as he removed his hand and felt my expression of triumph crumble. Here I thought he might be open to seeing reason, but it would take even more for him to realize this was a bad idea.

I sighed deeply, falling face-first onto the bed, and wishing that things would go back to how they were that morning when the only thing I had to worry about was watching Mariam and Trace fawn over each other. No, this new set of problems was much worse.

"This is really exciting if you think about it." Mariam had returned to check on me after Gabe announced to everyone downstairs that we were true mates and would be spending the night celebrating together privately. She rubbed my back through the robe that I still hadn't managed to change out of, using small circles to soothe me the way I did when she was sick or upset as a kid. "Gabe is great. Like, he really is the best, and he's someone you can grow to love. Especially when... you know... the mating bond is in place."

I groaned, the sound muffled by the pillow my face was buried into. Someone I could grow to love? What about swoony, instantaneous attraction? What about everything being so perfect that neither one of us could deny how right it was to be together? This wasn't my dream, not by a long shot.

You felt that attraction! We both did! My wolf pouted at me for trying to deny the legitimacy of the encounter earlier.

I scowled at her. *That's what happens when you're celibate for thirty-six years,* I reasoned. *Any amount of sexual tension probably feels that intense when you aren't used to any at all. And that still doesn't make up for the fact that he is basically a child and that he has the muscle tone of a toddler.*

That seemed to piss my wolf off even more. She glowered at me, exasperated with all my reasons and excuses for why she couldn't be with Gabe's wolf. None of them made any sense to her. That much was clear.

"I just think that you should give him a chance," Mariam continued, oblivious to my ongoing internal argument with my animal. "Gabe is so nurturing. I'm sure he'll give you the time you need to adjust."

Nurturing? Was *nurturing* what I really wanted from a mate? I stifled a laugh at the idea. Nurturing wasn't what made shifter men so hot and attractive. No, what made werewolf women swoon was the hot-blooded, dominant men who could throw them over their shoulders without a second thought. That's exactly what Mariam got. I bet she wouldn't be so happy with Trace if she had to wonder which one of them would win an arm-wrestling match.

"I don't want to go to dinner with him," I mumbled, flipping over to stare at the ceiling. "Can't you just tell him that I'm not interested? Tell him I've taken a vow of chastity or something."

Mariam grinned. "I could," she agreed. "And it wouldn't even be very far off from the truth, actually."

I threw the pillow at her and it felt surprisingly good when it made contact with her face. Avoiding sex until I found my true mate was NOT the same as taking a vow of chastity. In fact, it was what almost all shifters did, as it was a rule given to us by the moon goddess. Mariam was one of the few she-wolves who had ignored that rule, but in her mind, it made me a total prude.

"Okay, okay," she said with a sigh. "I get that you aren't interested in Gabe, but speaking from experience, sometimes things change and work out better than you expect them to when it comes to true mates,"

I rolled my eyes. "This is nothing like what happened with you and Trace, Mariam. Trace is… well, he is strong and tough and all the things that Dad was for Mom. He's your rock. It only makes sense that you're attracted to him."

The statement earned me a low growl from my sister. Male werewolves were known for being territorial when it came to their mates, but females weren't much better.

"That's not what I meant," I said quickly. "I'm not interested in Trace like that. I just meant that it makes sense that you would be into him. Gabe is nothing like Dad. He looks like he doesn't get enough sunlight or eat enough protein or something."

Mariam tilted her head back and gave a big belly laugh, her moment of jealousy quickly over and forgotten. "I can't argue with that. He does spend too much time inside the library looking up old werewolf bylaws, and he could probably use more fresh air, but maybe you could help him with that. You know, you could help him loosen up a little bit."

I shook my head. "Mariam, you of all people should remember exactly how tightly wound I am. After basically raising you, and getting a few thousand grey hairs doing it, by the way, I don't have it in me to try to raise another child. Especially one who is in his twenties."

"Hmmm..." Mariam tilted her head, considering my words. "I wonder if that's why the moon goddess has chosen you to be together. Gabe is nurturing as hell, and you have always been the caregiver. Maybe it's time someone took care of you for a change, Ella."

"Enough," I said, throwing my hands in the air. "It doesn't matter because I'm not going to do it. If this is the best the moon goddess can give me, maybe I'm better off choosing someone on my own. Or maybe I'd be better off having casual relationships like you did before meeting

Trace, Mare. Who even knows anymore?"

My wolf growled, indignant at that line of thinking. Mariam didn't look too pleased, either.

"You don't have to make a decision about everything right away, Ella, but please don't go and do something stupid. Gabe doesn't deserve that, and honestly, neither do you. I can promise you that sort of thing won't end well for either of you."

"Since when did you become the parent?" I huffed, sitting up and pulling my legs to my chest. "That sounds like something I would tell you if our roles were reversed."

"What can I say? I learned from the best."

She scooped me into her arms and tucked my head under her chin, just like I did when we were kids. Somehow, someway, she had become the wise bigger sister, and I had turned into the one with boy troubles.

Chapter 3

The next thing I knew, I was standing in the enormous kitchen helping Randy and his mate, Justine, make dinner. The alpha and beta couples took turns with the cooking responsibilities whenever possible, and tonight was their night. I could have stayed hidden upstairs, but after a while, I started to feel guilty that I wasn't helping out. The last thing I needed was for the pack to think that Mariam's only sister was a lazy bum.

And at least the huge ceremony-prepping crowd had dispersed, so I didn't have to face everyone who witnessed the debacle upstairs.

So now, I was doing my best to throw together a stir-fry for the alphas and betas to enjoy, assuming that Gabe was, in fact, serious about coming back and taking me out on the date. If he showed up, I had vowed to use the time together to talk him out of pursuing anything with me.

"This is amazing! You're doing great!" Justine said, tasting a bit of the sauce I was using to coat the vegetables. "Much better than Mariam when she first started living here."

Her mate growled from across the kitchen, warning her

to watch what she was saying. I tried and failed to hide my smile at her blunt honesty.

"Mariam has never been very lucky when it comes to cooking, I'm afraid. I actually help run the pack's bakery. Cooking and baking are a few of my favorite things, so I guess there was never a reason for her to learn when she lived with me."

Justine's eyes lit up. "Ooooh! You're a baker!? I can't wait for you to move to Tumblewild and—"

"Justine!" Randy said, exasperated. "I told you. No talking about any of that. Trace said it was a sensitive subject, remember?"

"I agreed to that before I knew she was a chef, Randy," Justine shot back. "That was before there were muffins and doughnuts and scones on the line."

"That's not all that's on the line if you don't cut it out."

My eyebrows rose slightly at the threat. Randy's face was dead-serious, and I thought I saw his hand twitch in anticipation of administering an impending spanking. I guess I shouldn't be that surprised. Mom and Dad had made it no secret that domestic discipline was essential to mated life, but witnessing it between people my age was something completely different.

"You're the one freaking her out with all the huffing and puffing, wolfman. Don't you remember how much that shit used to scare Mariam?"

Randy shot a concerned look my way, but I waved him off. "Mariam and I are about as different as two people can be. She didn't want the structure and the discipline, but I'm kind of looking forward to it."

I snapped my mouth shut and felt my cheeks glow

crimson. I hadn't meant to imply that I was looking forward to being spanked or anything. *Especially* not by Gabriel. I had only wanted to reassure Randy that he wasn't freaking me out.

But now it was too late. The admission hung in the air, and Justine's eyes danced with intrigue. She leaned forward on the counter, searching my ever-reddening face.

"Wait, you *want* your mate to discipline you?" Justine looked at Randy, silently asking him if he was hearing this. I could tell he had heard everything because he was looking at me rather thoughtfully like this had somehow made my presence infinitely more interesting. But for Justine, his only response was another weary sigh.

"Leave it, troublemaker," he said. "This conversation is over. You've mortified enough people for one day."

I thought for just a second that the sassy red-haired shifter might try her luck by ignoring her mate's command again, but in the end, she just shrugged and went back to setting the table. I shot Randy a grateful look that he acknowledged with a short nod. Above us, the large Tuscan-style clock let out a few chimes to indicate another hour had passed, and I began to breathe easier. Maybe Gabe had changed his mind about coming back this evening. Maybe he had—

The thought was interrupted by another bell going off, this one coming from the front door.

I had to admit Gabe cleaned up pretty well. Since leaving the alpha house that morning, he had showered and changed clothes, and it looked like he had even gotten a haircut. When I asked him about it, he blushed and fumbled a response about wanting to look more presentable than he had that morning. Gabe had even stopped and bought a fresh bouquet of roses, which Justine had promptly grabbed from him and put in some water.

It was all very sweet and charming but entirely unnecessary. I hadn't taken the arm he had offered me on the way to his car, and even now, several minutes into the drive to the restaurant, I wasn't exactly sure how to break the silence between us. A big part of me longed for the drive I had taken with Randy from the airport. That car ride felt like it was years ago. Had it really only been a few hours?

Gabe's hand flexed where it rested on the gearshift, drawing my attention to it. I could almost hear his thoughts, the ones telling him to reach over and stroke my exposed upper thigh.

Damn Mariam and her endless supply of scandalous dresses, I thought. *Damn me for not having anything fancy enough to wear and agreeing to try this one on.*

I wouldn't have known what to do if he actually tried to touch me (scream, pull away, hit him? Or maybe melt a little and savor the contact of another person? Or would that be crossing a line?), so it was good that his hands remained firmly where they were.

"So…." I cringed. *Real smooth, Ella.* "Where are we going to eat? Is it far?"

Those were reasonable questions and safe territory. It didn't give him any weird hope that this was going to work out, which was my biggest fear at the moment.

My stomach rumbled loudly in agreement, and I wanted

to die right then, at that specific moment. Gabe glanced at me apologetically and returned his attention back to the road. We had been traveling for about a half-hour already.

"Geez, I'm sorry, Ella," he said. "I didn't even think about how late it was getting. I wanted to take you somewhere special, and we don't have any fancy restaurants in Tumblewild. We're still a little way out from Flagstaff. Should we turn around and go to the diner instead? I have a reservation, but I can—"

"No, it's fine. This is fine," I said, cutting him off. If I was going to let Gabe down easy and not cause a rift between him and Mariam, I wasn't going to be a fussy date, too. I searched my mind for something -anything- else to say to keep the conversation going. "You've, um, gone there before on a date?"

You'd have thought I'd accused him of murdering a dozen puppies, the way he looked at me.

"Of course not! Ella, there's no one else. There has never been anyone else. I've been waiting for you." His hand moved now, but not toward me. Instead, he gripped the steering wheel tightly. "Has there been anyone else? You know, that you've… dated?"

He spat the last word out like it was poison. When I didn't answer immediately, Gabe shifted in his seat, clearly more uncomfortable with the silence now than he was earlier. I looked out the window and felt the slightest hint of a smile on my lips. If having former boyfriends upset Gabe this much, I may have just found a way to make him a lot less interested in pursuing anything with me.

The restaurant was gorgeous. I had never been to anything nearly as fancy as the steakhouse I was sitting in.

When the waiter asked about wine, Gabe looked at me to answer, and he seemed happy when I declined a glass. The moment was important somehow. Like it was a test, and I had passed. But I hadn't turned down the wine to pass some stupid test; I had never tasted alcohol and had no interest in starting now. I was especially thankful for that on a night like this, where having my wits about me was all the more critical.

Around us were humans on dates with a partner. Probably some of them were enjoying a night out with their spouses. I wrinkled my nose at the cold, impersonal word humans use to describe their chosen mates. They would never experience the magic of a true mate connection as they weren't shifters, but at least they could find another person to share their lives with. Maybe my love story would end up that way, too.

Gabe frowned at my reaction, misinterpreting my thoughts. "Is your steak okay?"

"What? Oh, yeah... it's great. Everything's great, Gabe. It was kind of you to take me here tonight." I brought my napkin to my mouth before folding it and setting it back on my lap, a nervous fidget. I steeled myself, ready to go in for the kill. "It reminds me of a place I went with this other male I was seeing."

That did the trick. If I wasn't paying attention, I would have missed it, but nope— the muscles in Gabe's neck tightened ever so slightly, and he swallowed a little too hard.

"I see," he replied, trying and failing to sound casual. "Was it serious, you with this other male?"

I chewed on my lip, and my werewolf growled a

warning to me. Ignoring her for the thousandth time that day, I answered with a response I hoped sounded off-handed and casual. "Yes, I guess it was. We considered becoming chosen mates."

He gave a short nod and turned back to his plate. He pushed the food around with his fork before abandoning it entirely and leaning back to look me in the eye.

"Was it just that one other guy, then? Anyone else I should know about?"

"Well, to tell you the truth, there were a few others. Patrick, Lance, Jason..." I started listing off the male werewolves Mariam had told me about, the ones she had been seeing before meeting Trace. The fact that I was claiming any of them was hilarious, considering that I, too, had been waiting for my true mate and had never so much as dipped my toes into the dating pool.

The shadow across Gabe's face changed. It didn't go away, but it turned into something different. Something unreadable.

Without another word, he reached into his wallet and withdrew a few hundred-dollar bills. He pushed away from the table and gestured for me to follow him. I raised my eyebrows but complied. *That was easier than I thought it would be.*

My wolf shook with rage or maybe fear. She could tell that the male werewolf was really pissed off, and it made her uncomfortable. *You should not have lied to our mate,* she accused.

I did it for us, so we could put all this nonsense to rest, go to the mating ceremony, and go back home. There wasn't really a way to explain this to her. Her instincts prevented her from seeing the situation from my perspective.

The she-wolf paced with nervous energy in the back of my mind. I could feel her contemplating forcing a shift, but I would shut that down fast. No matter how upset she was, we couldn't start sprouting fur and a snout in the parking lot of a human restaurant.

Back in the car, Gabe took a few deep breaths before starting the engine. He seemed lost in his own thoughts, and for the first time, I didn't feel the need to fill the silence with forced conversation. Instead, I watched the stars above as we drove in the silent darkness, counting as many as I could in the warm Arizona sky. I gasped aloud as one took off. A shooting star, on tonight of all nights.

"What did you wish for?"

The soft-spoken question coming from the driver's seat startled me. What would I wish for? Before today, that answer would have been simple. I would have wished for my true mate to show up and for my life, my *real* life, to finally begin. But now, I was tempted to wish for the exact opposite. I wanted things to go back to the way they were.

When it became clear that I was not going to answer, Gabe filled the silence again. "I've always heard that you shouldn't tell people your wish, but I don't think that applies to us. True mates shouldn't have secrets from each other."

I felt, rather than saw, his long sideways glance. "But then that begs the question, mate, of why you decided to lie to me tonight."

My chest constricted. "I don't know what you mean," I replied evenly.

"You don't think I know about some of Mariam's sordid

tales? The names of a few of her *friends*? We lived together for a month, Ella. She's kind of my best friend."

"Oh." I should have come up with some different names, some random werewolves back home. I hadn't thought Mariam would tell Gabe anything about her past lovers, but it was too late to correct the mistake now. I was caught.

"Yeah. Oh," Gabe repeated. "Mariam also mentioned that, unlike her, you have always been extremely chaste. Thanks for that, by the way. I think every male hopes his true mate would wait for him."

"No problem," I mutter under my breath. He kept going like he hasn't heard me, though I'm sure his werewolf hearing picked up my response.

"But now we have a problem, and I'm not sure how to handle it, Ella. If you would just accept our bond, I would already have you over my knee for telling a lie. You would have your punishment, and then we'd be done with it, but you're still insisting that we're not mates. Going as far as to make up ridiculous stories, as if that would make me not want you."

I sucked in a breath. How was I supposed to respond to that? My wolf had a few ideas, one of which included me crawling onto his lap and stripping off all my clothes. I wasn't going to entertain those thoughts, though. I banished the images from my mind.

"Listen, Gabe," I started. "I'm sorry I lied to you, but it doesn't change anything. I'm leaving as soon as Mariam's ceremony is over. We aren't a good fit, and this conversation proves that more than anything."

Gabe didn't answer, which all but confirmed my line of thinking. I didn't want a mate who was afraid to throw me over his knee. Gabe, with his calm, cool, boyish looks, embodied everything that made for a good friend, but that was all. If I ever did mate with someone, it would be because there was something raw and powerful between us. It would be with someone I could actually see myself submitting to. *Just like Mariam and Trace*, I thought again, for maybe the hundredth time that day. *Just like Mom and Dad.*

When I first arrived at Tumblewild, I had been dreading all the mating ceremony preparations and bearing witness to my sister sucking the face off Trace Everett, but it really wasn't all that bad. Face-sucking aside, being in the ceremony kept me busy enough that there wasn't really time to think about Gabe or the eerily quiet ride home.

Okay- that's a lie. It *almost* kept me busy enough not to think about it. It wasn't my fault that Gabe's face kept flashing in my mind. My wolf was restless and agitated; every time I pictured him, she turned a little wilder. Finally, somewhere between helping Mariam with her dress alterations and having Justine practice doing my eye makeup, I couldn't ignore the urge to shift any longer.

"I'm sorry. My wolf...I just have to go."

My rushed exit would have made no sense to a human, but everyone nearby seemed to understand that I was on edge. Justine even gave me a knowing smile as I bolted from the room, almost like she knew why I had to shift and had been wondering how long I would be able to hold off on doing it.

I barely made it to the woods lining the yard of the alpha

house when she came bursting forth. My clothes were completely shredded, but there was nothing I could do to avoid it. I had ignored the animal for too long, especially considering the whole true mate situation, and now I would pay for it in new clothing.

My senses exploded like they always do during a shift. My heart beat in time with the wolf's footsteps, racing faster as she gained speed and zigzagged through the trees. I could feel her savoring the feel of the dirt beneath her paws and her delight in the open, unfenced space around us. Back home, pack lands were surrounded on all sides by housing developments, leaving only a compound of homes, buildings, and empty land for pack members to enjoy. Jeremy had forbidden anyone from shifting and running through human territory because he was afraid someone would mistake one of our kind for a regular wolf and kill it. But that didn't stop some younger, more adventurous wolves from sneaking out and letting loose anyway. I had never understood their desire to run outside the community gates, but now I could absolutely see the appeal.

My wolf made the loop around the alpha property a few times, investigating the scents other Tumblewild pack members had left behind. From the array of fresh tracks, it was clear that the alpha property was available for others in the pack to use as they pleased. My wolf gave a rumble of happiness at how communal this pack seemed. Dark Claw wasn't the most conservative pack, but Jeremy would never allow other pack members around his home without an invitation or reason for being there.

The thought fled from my mind as I was assaulted with

a new scent. Or, rather, a scent that was becoming more and more familiar over the last twenty-four hours.

A nearby bush rustled, and out from it sprang a brown wolf with grey markings on its chest. My wolf recognized him at once and folded herself into an embarrassing puppy bow. Her tail swung in the air, trying to tempt him into playing with her.

The invitation worked, and Gabe's wolf leaped at her. She dodged him easily and took off deep into the wooded hills. She did her best to outrun him, and when that didn't work, she tried to outsmart him by doubling back on her trail. To her surprise, he managed to stick right behind her, not once falling for her sneaky tricks.

When it felt like the air was going to burst from her lungs and she couldn't run any longer, my wolf collapsed beneath the shade of an old juniper tree. Gabe's wolf wasted no time nuzzling up to her and lightly clamping down on her exposed throat, an act of dominance that surprised me. Maybe his wolf wasn't as passive as the man himself.

Chapter 4

I hadn't meant to fall asleep. It had just been so comfortable in the shade of the tree that I had completely lost myself in relaxing under it. And so had Gabe, it seemed.

I woke with a start at the realization that the sun was setting, and the air was growing cooler. I sat up, horribly human and naked, with leaves sticking to my butt and twigs in my hair.

"Just when I thought you couldn't get more beautiful," a voice rumbled behind me.

I gasped and covered myself with my hands. I had naively hoped Gabe was still asleep, allowing me to shift back without being noticed. Of course, he was staring at me instead, with an intensity like he was trying to memorize the entire landscape of my body.

"Can you just look somewhere else, please?" I hissed. "I'm going to shift and leave as soon as I can."

Gabe laughed, causing me to frown. "There's no way I would miss a chance to see you naked, mate. Especially when I have a feeling that it might not happen again for a while."

For a while? "Try never," I spat back, heat rising in my cheeks. Try as I might to summon my wolf from inside, she was pretending to be asleep, too.

Traitor, I whispered to her. Was she really going to make me walk back to the alpha house naked?

"Is there a problem?" Gabe asked, his words seeping with humor. I glared at him. I was tempted to sneak a look lower than his face but at the same time I didn't dare to take a glance. The curiosity, or perhaps the struggle, must have been written on my face.

"I'm yours to enjoy, too, Ella," he said, reclining further against the tree. If I wasn't already blushing, that would have been enough to do it.

"I'm good," I said between gritted teeth. "You know, if you were as great a guy as Mariam said, you might give me a little privacy or shift back yourself, you know?"

"If your sister was here, I would do either of those things in a heartbeat, Ella." Gabe's words were as smooth as silk, and I found myself leaning toward him. He smiled and leaned in, as well. "But she's not. You are. And I'm not going to just be a 'nice guy' to you, mate."

I chewed on my lower lip, not sure how to respond to that. The movement caught his eye, and his stare became heated. I didn't need access to his thoughts to know that they were quickly turning in a different direction.

I have to get out of here.

Suddenly, having to walk back to the house naked was the least of my worries. There was a strong pull to crawl back into Gabe's arms and snuggle up against him. It was undeniable, no matter how much I wanted to say it wasn't true. I carefully stood and began the trek back up the hill.

I was honestly surprised by how easily he was letting me walk away without so much as another comment on my nudity or even a regular, G-rated goodbye. I glanced back at the tree, hoping that he wasn't watching the sway of my hips as I walked, but he was already gone. Frowning, I turned to continue on the path but instead found myself face-to-face with him again.

"Goddess!" I grabbed at my chest. He wasn't literally giving me a heart attack, but it was startling, to say the least. His footsteps had been completely silent. Or maybe I had been lost in my own head and just wasn't paying attention. Either way, a fully naked Gabriel now stood in my way, leaving me no choice but to engage with him again.

I kept my eyes above the belt, but this time it wasn't as hard to do. What caught my eye were the clothes in his hands. Apparently, his wolf hadn't forced a shift like mine, so he had a chance to remove his clothing before sprouting fur. As I came closer, he thrust his shirt into my hands.

"Here," he said. "If one of us has to be topless, it should probably be me. My wolf doesn't appreciate the alternative when you'll be around other males."

I didn't want to encourage his wolf's possessive nature, but I also didn't want the whole house to see me nude. Without a word, I grabbed the shirt and pulled it over my head. I crossed my arms under my substantial breasts, wishing that he would somehow magically produce a spare bra, as well. Together, we walked back to the house in companionable silence. When we neared the front door and finally did speak, it happened as a jumble, both talking at the same time.

Gabe: "So, I'll pick you up in an hour for dinner?"

Me: "I'll give Mariam your shirt, so you don't have to stop by again."

He narrowed his eyes at me, causing me to glare back.

"Really?" I demanded. "You didn't have enough *dinner* last night?"

He cracked a grin at that and quickly tugged me to him. "I'll never have enough *dinner* with you, Ella," he whispered. Somehow, he made that simple statement sound like an invitation directly into his bed.

My mouth went dry, both at the innuendo and at his arm hooked around my waist. My nipples puckered under the shirt, happy to be pressed against his bare chest. Somewhere lower, I felt myself tighten at the contact.

I pushed away from him, allowing the space between us to calm my beating heart.

"I'm eating here tonight, Gabe. And I'll be busy for the next few days, too, so don't bother stopping by." I could have ended with that and gone inside, but I was on a roll; the words just kept pouring out of my stupid mouth. There was nothing I could do to stop it. "I'm here for the mating ceremony and haven't really done anything to help Mariam. And it's the day after tomorrow! So, yeah, I'm too busy. I'll see you… around."

His eyebrows raised, and the sides of his mouth twitched to form a grin. A very appealing grin. He closed the space I had created and leaned his body against mine. My wolf rumbled her approval as our hips made contact. It took every ounce of self-control I had in me not to grind against him. *When did I turn into such a--*

"You know what, Ella?" Gabe whispered into my ear,

putting any other thoughts I had on hold. "I think you've forgotten that I'm going to be part of this ceremony, too. We'll be seeing each other a lot over the next few days, *dinner* or no *dinner*."

He was close, *so close*, to brushing his lips against mine. I could feel the heat from his breath stirring in the cool early evening air. Thankfully, he was the one who pulled back this time. I'm not sure I would have been able to. My wolf's encouragement to grab his face and kiss him wasn't helping, that's for sure.

With a glimmer in his eye, he gave me a short nod and another heartbreaking smile before turning and walking back to his car, hands in his pockets. His shoulders looked relaxed, matching the self-assured saunter. I bet he was enjoying the feel of my eyes on him. With no shirt, he was something to look at, even without having the huge muscles male werewolves were known for. His form was lean, more refined. He was almost... beautiful.

It took me a shameful amount of time to snap out of my trance and rush to the front door, but when I finally did, it felt as if one problem had been traded for another. It sounded like he wasn't going to push for another dinner date, but what exactly did he mean about spending more time around here?

I kicked off my shoes and glanced into the front room, groaning as I took in the sight of everyone staring at me. Trace and Randy had matching smirks on their faces, clearly amused by something, but Mariam and Justine looked downright giddy.

"We saw you," Justine gushed, clapping her hands with excitement. "We saw you both through the window. It was so romantic. You, wearing his shirt and basically simulating sex in the driveway. Get it, girl!"

"I can't believe you're mated to Gabe," Mariam added. "It's just so surreal but so perfect at the same time."

I found my way up the stairs, not wanting to listen to any of it another minute longer. I closed the bedroom door and slid down onto the floor, much the same way I had after arriving from the airport. This was crazy. Some version of a sick joke. All I needed was a hot bath and a good night's sleep. Maybe I would dream and come up with a new plan by the morning.

I soaked in the tub and curled up under the sheets, too tired to care about missing dinner or that it was still way too early to go to bed. Sleep would make everything go by faster, and that's exactly what I wanted.

"Wake up, Ella."

I groaned, rebelling against the bright light in the room and the sound of Mariam trying to coax me awake. There had been many mornings like this but usually they were completely reversed, with Mariam's head buried in the pillow and my voice threatening that she was going miss the school bus if she didn't wake up. Had so much time really passed since then? It didn't feel like that long ago.

"Come on," she pleaded. She grabbed one of the many extra pillows off the bed and began beating me with it.

I groaned louder before sitting up in a huff. "Fine, you win."

"I always do," she said, smiling sweetly. "But seriously, you've been asleep forever. The morning's basically over, and I need your help."

"You need my help?" I asked cautiously. "With what?"

Mariam gaped at me. "I don't know, Ella. Maybe with the mating ceremony that's happening here *tomorrow*."

"Oh yeah," I said, sheepish. I had spent the night tossing and turning, worrying about what to do about the whole true mate thing. I finally passed out in the mid-morning, and now my mind felt fuzzy from a lack of restful sleep. "Um…yeah, of course. What do you need me to do?"

"Like, a million things. Everything." She leaned back against the headboard, chewing on her lip the same way I do when I'm debating what to say next. I waited for her to continue, knowing there would be more. "Look, I've been trying to give you space since the whole Gabe thing happened, but I also really need you. I want you to be in the ceremony, but if you want to just sit it out, if it's too much—"

"No, I can do it. I want to do it." I cringed at my own selfishness that she would even need to offer me an out like this. Mariam and I were all each other had. Without me, there wouldn't be another family member to stand by her side at the ceremony. "I'm sorry I've been so preoccupied. You will have my full, undivided attention starting now. Promise."

Mariam beamed at me.

"So, what's the first order of business then, boss?"

"First," she said. "You brush your teeth. Seriously, your morning breath is lethal, Ella. Then meet me downstairs in the living room so we can go over everything for tomorrow.

I threw a pillow at her.

A half-hour later, I was downstairs dressed, brushed, and ready to help with whatever Mariam needed. My eyes widened slightly at the whiteboard wheeled in front of the couch. It had a million words scribbled all over it. Thankfully, most of them were either crossed out or had a checkmark next to them.

"Okay, as you can see, pretty much all the decorating and food has already been handled. The music was finalized yesterday. Everyone's outfits are good. If yours is okay, that is. You never got back about that, so I assumed the dress fits."

I nodded. Not responding when she asked about the dress hadn't been entirely intentional. I had meant to text her, but I kept putting it off until it was practically time to board the flight.

"Good," she said, picking up the dry-erase marker. "That just leaves your speech, some loose ends with Jeremy, and the rehearsal tonight. Have you got everything figured out?"

I swallowed hard. Of course, I was aware tradition demanded that I make some kind of speech on Mariam's behalf. It should be our father telling everyone about how wonderful she is, about how perfect Trace is for her. But with dad and mom gone, the responsibility was mine now.

"What loose ends with Jeremy? Is he here?"

Mariam frowned at my non-answer, but her expression quickly changed to a smirk. "He texted late last night and said he would be flying in today. Something about Neil stepping in while he was gone."

I rolled my eyes. Mariam had always hated Neil, the beta of Dark Claw, and she made no attempt to hide her distaste for him. "I'm sure he will do fine acting as pack leader while Jeremy is here. What's wrong with Neil anyway? What'd he ever do to you?"

"Nothing. He's just... Neil."

"Well, he can't exactly help being himself, Mariam," I said.

"I'm not saying he can help it," she snapped. "He's just not the best, that's all."

Neil certainly wasn't the most popular member of the Dark Claw pack, that's for sure. Whatever Mariam saw that made her dislike him, she wasn't the only one. When Jeremy had taken over the pack and announced Neil as his beta, there had been a lot of moaning and groaning, especially among the shifters our age. Even in school when we were kids, everyone had pretty much steered clear of Neil, and he acted like a loner. Mariam didn't remember those days, of course. We were practically ready to graduate, then she was still running around in diapers. So that begged the question, what could she possibly have against him? As far as I knew, they hadn't even really spoken to each other.

"What time is the rehearsal?" I asked, ready to change the subject. "Who's going to be here?"

Mariam gave me a sideways smile. "Why do you want to know? Anyone in particular you're looking forward to seeing?"

"Ugh, no," I groaned. "Tell me he's not coming."

"Hey, what's wrong with Gabe, anyway? He's, like, the best guy around. Except for Trace, but he doesn't count." Mariam paused, glancing around the room before whispering. "Honestly, sometimes he's even a better guy than Trace."

"I heard that." A disembodied male voice bellowed from the kitchen, though there wasn't any malice in his tone, and Trace didn't emerge to confront her, so he was probably joking. Nevertheless, Mariam and I both cringed, her for being caught and me for the awkward discussion being overheard. Heightened werewolf hearing was more trouble than it was worth most of the time.

"He's nice, don't get me wrong, Mare. But 'nice' isn't exactly what I'm hoping for in a mate."

Mariam raised her eyebrows. "Let me get this straight. Gabe is nice, so you don't want him? What do you want? Some arrogant asshole?"

"Probably, but this one's taken." Trace appeared in the doorway, leaning against the stone column as he gazed at his mate. I would have thought that Mariam would be annoyed at the interruption and chew him out, but instead, she gave him a softer look and nodded her agreement.

"It's true, Ella," she said. "We're fresh out of assholes now. You should take your pick of the nice guys, and my vote is for you to settle down with Gabe. Especially since, you know, the whole true mate thing is a pretty big deal to you."

"And here I thought it was a big deal to you, too," Trace huffed. He crossed the room and scooped Mariam up, holding her close and ignoring her flailing hands. She squealed and pretended to try to get away, but it was clear that she loved his attention.

This was precisely the kind of scene that I had been worried about seeing. The two of them were so in love, so happy together, and I knew that I would be bitter about not having a true mate of my own. But now that the moment had actually come, I wasn't jealous of not having a true mate; I was jealous that mine probably wouldn't be able to lift me off the ground with the same kind of ease.

We went running with him. He is strong and capable, my wolf insisted. She didn't care that Gabe wasn't Mr. Brawny. Whatever he was, she thought he was perfect.

She could continue thinking whatever she wanted. I already knew my plans, and they didn't include moving to Tumblewild and setting up a house with Gabriel.

I left the two lovebirds to continue doing whatever they were doing (not making out exactly, but something close enough to it that I didn't want to stick around and watch) and decided to leave for another run. The sun was out, and those gorgeous trees were calling to me again. This time, at least my wolf wasn't bursting to get out, and I was able to duck around the side of the house for privacy and change out of my clothes before shifting.

Down below in the grassy open space, pack members were setting up chairs and changing stations for the ceremony the next day. My wolf crept around the outside of the perimeter, not wanting to disturb their work or draw attention to herself. She was very much aware that they belonged to another pack, and no matter how many times I assured her that Tumblewild meant us no harm, she still refused to let her guard down with anyone other than Mariam.

And our mate, she reminded me.

Yeah. Him, too.

I let her guide the run again, reveling in her excitement over the vast terrain. This time, she decided to run by the road toward downtown. Of course, it didn't matter if anyone saw us, with the whole of Tumblewild being werewolves, too. But it felt odd that she would rather move toward the buildings and cars she wanted to avoid back home.

She stopped and sniffed the air every few miles. It wasn't unusual for her to do that, and out here in rural Arizona, doing so might even earn her a snack like a tasty rabbit or a fresh raccoon. It wasn't until we had reached Town Hall that I realized she wasn't hunting; she had been trying to track Gabe. And if his strong scent was any indication that he was nearby, she had been successful.

Chapter 5

What the hell? My wolf was doing a great job of ignoring me and continued on with her search like she hadn't heard a word of my protests. Short of forcing her to shift back, there was little I could do to make her take us back home if she refused to listen. Of course, forcing a shift here would also mean that I would be naked in front of a whole bunch of strangers, and I would rather avoid that, if possible.

This is the last time I let you take over, I huffed.

Her ears flickered in the wind. Gabe's scent was strong here, and she stood quietly listening to catch his voice if he was nearby. After several minutes, she began scenting the air again to see if she could track him to a more specific area.

She led us to a small cafe down the street where Gabe sat in a booth next to the front window. She gave a full-toothed, wolfy grin at seeing our mate enjoying his lunch. I rolled my eyes, ready to be really pissed off at her if he looked up and caught us watching him.

Her relaxed demeanor shifted when the pretty waitress stopped to refill his drink. She leaned forward to whisper something into his ear, and rather than recoil or push her away as any typical mated male would, Gabe just laughed and whispered something back to her. It was hard to tell from a distance, but it looked like he even leaned into her touch when she nudged his shoulder playfully.

My wolf growled, enraged at the sight. For some unexplainable reason, I felt my blood boil, too. It didn't mean I wanted Gabe for myself. It couldn't mean that. But I guess it meant I didn't want the waitress to touch him like that. I *really* didn't want her whispering things into his ear, and seeing him do it back to her was almost enough to make me shift back into our human form, naked or not.

We need to leave. Let's go back to the alpha house, I pleaded with the blood-thirsty wolf. If we hurry, we'll still have a little time to run through the trees before the rehearsal.

But no amount of prodding would sway her. She sat there, focused on the man in the diner, waiting to see what would happen. She wanted to know if the woman was coming back and how he would handle it. For the first time, I felt her questioning him and his worthiness, but she refused to form the thoughts into words. Her emotions ran tight, and I was afraid that, at any moment, they would snap under the strain.

I let out a huge sigh of relief when a different woman appeared to give Gabe his check. This one was older, and while her body language was friendly enough, it never crossed the line into flirting. We watched together as he picked up his messenger bag and headed for the door. He paused as a gust of wind came from above, throwing our scent across the street directly to him.

Let's go before he sees us, I begged. For the first time since leaving the house, my wolf complied and slinked off into the shadows. It was clear that seeing the woman with Gabe had shaken her a lot. Flirting with the waitress was not what she considered worthy mate behavior, and frankly, it wasn't something I would be thrilled about, either. I was stunned to see Gabe acting that way since he made such a big deal about not having any other infatuations or love interests. Had he been lying that whole night just to try to get me to accept the mating bond with him? That didn't seem like something Gabe would do. Not if he was the kind of guy Mariam thought he was, anyway.

I sighed. All these thoughts and contradictions were making my head spin. I wanted to hide away upstairs again, but I had promised Mariam that I would help her out today. I was already breaking that promise a little bit with how long this run was taking.

Getting back to the house felt a hundred times longer than the run over. Possibly because now we were both burdened with what had happened. After pulling my clothes on and stumbling back into the house, I was so distracted that I almost ran smack into Randy, who was carrying several boxes of fresh red roses.

"Here- let me help you," I said apologetically. I grabbed a few boxes from the top. He murmured his thanks, and I followed him back down to the clearing in the backyard.

It truly was beautiful. Lanterns had been arranged around the wooden platform. The ceremony would include a pack-wide shift, so there weren't any chairs in the audience. Instead, pillows and yards of soft fabric were tied down to give the guests something to sit on while the vows were being recited. Everything was deep cream or red, nicely offsetting the dark green grass and trees surrounding us. Whoever Mariam had hired to help with coordinating the deco had done a great job.

Randy was setting the roses into large glass vases, so I brought the ones I had over to him and began doing the same. I stepped back to admire the bouquets when it was finished, but he caught my eye instead. Randy was a mated male shifter. Maybe he would know if Gabe's actions had crossed a line.

"Randy?"

"Yeah?" He was distracted and out of his depth trying to arrange the flowers. I took a deep breath to gather my nerve and broach the topic.

"Um…as a mated male werewolf, would you ever, you know… flirt with someone else?" Randy stilled instantly at the question. My cheeks flamed red, and I regretted saying anything at all.

"What?" He glanced at me and then began rearranging the flowers more aggressively as though they might be able to save him from the conversation. "Listen, Ella, you're a nice girl and all, but I'm not--"

"Oh, goddess, that is NOT what I meant. Never mind, forget I said anything, please. Please. Please." I just kept repeating that last word as I turned and walked back to the house. For one horrifying moment, I thought he was going to follow me, but when I glanced over my shoulder, he had gone back to manhandling the roses. I probably wouldn't be able to look him in the eye for a long time.

"Where have you been? You promised you would help with the rest of the planning today." Mariam caught me as soon as I crossed the threshold of the large front doors.

"I was helping Randy bring your roses down," I said,

cringing at the awkwardness I had left in my wake and the bitter taste of the half-truth on my lips. "What else do you need me to do?"

Mariam glanced at the woman with the clipboard on her right, the same one who had been helping her in the madness when I first arrived at the house. "Jess, what else do we need to get done before the rehearsal?"

Jess. I scrunched my face, trying to place the name. Mariam had said something about this person before, but I hadn't paid close enough attention. Maybe this was another friend she had made in Tumblewild?

"We need to set up the dining area on the veranda, and then we should be good to go," she said, eyeing the clipboard. "Just in time, too. The rehearsal guests should be arriving in an hour."

"Wait. Do I need to change?" I asked, glancing down at the jeans I was wearing. They were the same pair that I had left outside for the better part of the day, so more than a few twigs and dirt smudges were clearly visible. Mariam's glare told me I shouldn't have even asked. "Right. I'll change, then meet you on the veranda for any last-minute things you might need."

"Fine. As long as that clothes change includes a shower," she said. "I don't know where you've been all day, but you smell awful."

———

I had never been more grateful to take a hot shower. The run to town and back had left me completely exhausted and more than a little sweaty. The water soothed my tight muscles, and the body wash cut through the woodsy smell, but nothing helped to relieve the pit of anxiety in my stomach.

My wolf felt it, too, possibly even more than I did. She was fidgety, pacing around in the corner of my mind. Her faith in Gabe was shaken, and she wasn't handling that well. I felt bad for her, but there wasn't anything I could do to help. Maybe this would be the proof she needed that Gabe wasn't a great match for us.

For the first time, she didn't try to argue when the thought crossed my mind, a testament to the level of doubt she was feeling about our mate.

I switched off the water and wrapped myself in a fuzzy towel, scrunching my hair dry as I walked. Mariam, or someone at her direction, had laid out an elegant black dress on the bed. Unlike the one from the date, this dress actually covered my thighs almost down to my knees. The cut of the bodice was similarly modest yet appealing, with sheer tule covering what would have been bare skin in a more revealing outfit. I took several minutes in the mirror, admiring how it hugged my frame without making me feel insecure. I loved it.

True to my word, I arrived on the veranda just in time to help set out the glassware and plates. The caterers were shifters, too; their scent gave them away as much as the wolf emblem on their aprons.

I paused when Mariam joined us outside. She was a vision, and it took me a second to recognize the woman before me as my younger sister. Trace couldn't keep his eyes off her, either, and for good reason. Her short cream dress was trendy and glamorous, something I could never pull off, but she made it look…perfect.

Her eyes widened when she saw me, too. "Ella, that is… I mean, that dress looks perfect on you. Where did you get it?"

I frowned. "It was on my bed when I went to take a shower. I thought you had left it for me."

"Nope, not me. Maybe you have a secret admirer." Her eyes twinkled at the idea, but I just shook my head.

"I already have more than I want in that department right now," I said. "It must have been Justine. I'm sure you've already told her how hopeless I am at getting dressed up. She probably wanted to help."

The guilty look that crossed my sister's face confirmed that I was correct on that count.

The evening was ready to begin. Thankfully, this wasn't a huge dinner, nothing like the celebration planned for tomorrow. Tonight was just an opportunity to discuss everything that was going to happen with those who had roles in the ceremony and do a quick practice run before enjoying a meal together. If I had it my way, the actual mating ceremony would be more like this and less like a huge production. But maybe that was why the moon goddess had chosen Mariam as a mate for the alpha of Tumblewild and not me; my sister clearly didn't mind hosting the massive event.

Jess, Randy, and Justine were already in the house somewhere. Jeremy was next to arrive, followed by a group of male werewolves I didn't know and one I did. My heart raced when Gabe stepped out onto the oversized porch. He scanned the group mingling by the outdoor fireplace, but his gaze stopped when he found me. He took his time looking me up and down, leaving me feeling unbelievably exposed, even in the conservative dress.

I wanted to run and hide somewhere, but there was nowhere for me to go. I stayed frozen instead, drink in hand, as he came to join me. When he was close enough, he dipped his head low to rumble in my ear.

"I knew it would look beautiful on you, but I had no idea it would drive me out of my mind."

My thoughts were scattered, and it took longer than I would like to admit to understand what he was talking about. Of course. The dress.

"You bought this for me?" I looked down at the outfit that had given me so much pleasure. Knowing that Gabe had selected it tainted it somehow. I wanted to rip it off my body and throw it into the woods, especially with the way he was leering at me. I didn't want to give him an ounce of satisfaction. "If I had known it was from you, I wouldn't have worn it."

Gabe blinked at my cold words, and I felt a chill run down my spine. Did I really just say that out loud?

"I don't understand," he said slowly. "Have I done something to offend you, Ella? Do you not like the dress?"

"This isn't about the dress. I don't want you picking out clothes for me. I especially don't want you in my bedroom or looking at me like *that*." My hands shook, but my voice remained steady. I was really proud of myself for not faltering with him standing so close.

Gabe narrowed his eyes. "I think this is a conversation we need to have in private, mate. It certainly isn't the type of discussion I want during Mariam's dinner party, but we will have it there if necessary. You might think that I'm a pushover because you haven't seen me go crazy like Trace, but that doesn't mean that you aren't in danger of being put over my knee for rudeness."

I felt my confidence falter, but then I reinforced it with some heady indignation. Who did he think he was, trying to boss me around after flirting with the waitress at the cafe? "You have it all wrong if you think I would ever allow that to happen, Gabe. Let's not ruin Mariam and Trace's evening and just try to stay away from each other, okay?"

I downed the last of my sparkling water and moved to join Justine, feigning interest in her conversation. I could feel Gabe's glare on the back of my neck, and every instinct in me was screaming to run back and try to make things right with him, but I remained firmly planted where I stood.

Soon enough, Trace called everyone over to the ceremony site, and I continued to use Justine and Randy as a barrier from Gabe. If they caught on to it, they never said a thing, though Randy was pointedly avoiding any eye contact with me, probably because of our conversation earlier. Usually, I would have been right there with him, but I had more pressing concerns than being hung up on an awkward misunderstanding. Like, for example, the male werewolf on the other side of the room who was getting angrier with each passing moment I ducked away from him.

Trace and Mariam took their places in the center of the platform, with Jeremy standing in the middle between them. Justine and Randy moved to stand on the other side of Trace, leaving me alone next to Mariam. Alone, that is, until Gabe joined me at her side.

"What are you doing?" I hissed at him.

Gabe shrugged. "When Mariam found out that we were true mates, she asked me to stand with you. That's tradition, I believe. Including siblings and their mates in the ceremony." He nodded to where Randy stood next to Justine on the other side of the platform.

I struggled to speak and come up with a reason why he shouldn't be here, but I stopped when I realized that everyone was staring at me. Jeremy raised an eyebrow, and we exchanged a glance.

He was clearly surprised to see me with someone, and I couldn't blame him. I think everyone in Dark Claw had expected me to die an old maid.

I gave up the fight and shrugged, returning my attention to Mariam and Trace. Jeremy gave a brief rundown of his part, but I wasn't paying attention. Soon enough, Gabe was elbowing me, prompting me to speak.

Of course. This was the part of the ceremony where I would speak on behalf of Mariam.

"I'm saving it for tomorrow," I murmured, hoping that would buy me more time to come up with what to say. The fib worked, and they moved on to Justine's speech to Trace. She must have said something funny because everyone chuckled.

Finally, at the end of the ceremony, Trace and Mariam made their vows to each other. Tomorrow, this would be when they would shift and lead the pack in a run through the woods. Mariam would officially be an alpha of Tumblewild, and I would hopefully be leaving for the airport to buy a new plane ticket and catch the redeye back home.

The meal afterward had Gabe and me sitting next to each other, of course. We were joined by Justine and Randy and a few of the other male werewolves who turned out to be pack council members. I wondered idly where their females were or if they were unmated males. My wolf couldn't care less about anyone else at the table. She was desperately trying to find a way to connect with our mate again, almost willing to forget everything that had happened at the diner.

Well, that made one of us, because I wasn't forgetting anything.

Underneath the table, Gabe's hand was firmly planted on my leg. I had initially tried to scoot away from him, and for a minute, it felt like he was giving in, but then he changed his mind and gripped the fabric of my dress tighter. I could have put up a bigger fight, but that would have drawn attention to us and away from the happy couple. So instead, we sat in silence with me pretending that I couldn't feel his thumb caressing my skin, only the thin layer of fabric between us.

Chapter 6

As soon as the dishes were cleared away, I stood quickly and excused myself to the restroom. I was fast enough that Gabe didn't even have a chance to argue, though I had a feeling he wanted to. I ignored the bathrooms downstairs in favor of escaping to my room. I needed space and a chance to think about what to tell Gabe when he inevitably wanted to talk about my sour attitude.

In the corner of the bedroom was a lounging chair. I slumped into it, running my fingers over the intricately carved wooden frame. It was beautiful, and probably really expensive. But it wasn't home, and I missed my living room's outdated, simple furniture. Hopefully, it would only be a matter of hours before I was back in my favorite recliner with a book and cup of tea in hand.

We need to talk with our mate and settle this issue. My wolf was coming to Gabe's defense again. Or, at least, she was prompting me to give him a chance to explain himself. I sighed, not wanting to argue with her about it.

It was really peaceful in this room, quiet enough that I started to nod off, but then I was startled awake at the sound of footsteps in the hallway. They were masculine and decidedly clipped. Whoever it was wasn't happy. I jumped as the door handle turned, already knowing who would be on the other side.

"Ella," he said, my name sounding both like a promise and a threat. "You've been gone for a while. Most of the guests are leaving, and I'm sure you want to say goodbye."

I blinked. I didn't know those council members and Justine and Randy wouldn't be leaving. I was about to disagree when the slight smile tugged at his otherwise serious expression. He was making fun of me.

"So, I'm not the most social person," I said, my arms wrapping around my chest defensively. "I barely know anyone here, so I'm sure they won't be heartbroken that I decided to come up and rest for a while."

"No, you're right. The council members probably didn't even notice you leaving, but I think Mariam was a little sad to see you go." He entered the room and crossed the space without waiting for an invitation. I stiffened as he took a seat next to me.

"I'm sure she'll understand when I explain that I'm not feeling well. I should rest up and save my energy for tomorrow, anyway. That's when she'll really be depending on me."

Gabe nodded but didn't seem convinced. I sighed, frustrated that he couldn't take a hint. I wasn't up for company, especially his.

"So…I'll see you at the ceremony tomorrow, Gabe. Have a good night." I tried standing and walking to the door to show him out, but the minute I was on my feet, Gabe was there with me. He grabbed my wrists and tugged them above my head, backing me gently against the wall.

My heart raced so fast that I thought it would beat out of my chest.

"Ella," he whispered again, saying it in that same magical way that was enough to make me weak at the knees. "What am I going to do with you? You're driving me crazy. You know that?"

Did I know that? Did it matter?

"Gabe," I said, my voice strained. I tried to remain firm in my resolve, but the pressure from his hips grinding into mine was difficult to ignore. "I'm going home tomorrow. Just…can you just give me some space?"

"No," he said simply. With that, he lowered his head and brought his lips close to mine. My eyelids fluttered, and I knew there was no way I could stop him if he wanted to kiss me. Even I, the ice queen, according to Mariam, was melting.

We moved at once, together, so it was impossible to tell who started the kiss. I take that back— he was thoroughly, completely kissing me, and I was letting him. He licked the seam of my mouth, and I opened for him without hesitation, eager to feel more of him. Eager to have him inside of me.

He growled low in his chest, clearly pleased with my enthusiastic compliance. His hands wrapped tightly around my waist, drawing me closer. He traveled lower to cup and squeezed my butt through the dress.

Mariam would say ass. I should grow up and just say ass, too.

He grabbed my ass. There. Much better.

I had never felt so wild and out of control, but I didn't want it to end. I slanted my mouth and brought my hands up to Gabe's hair, gripping it at the roots to keep him in place. Gabe nipped at my lips, maybe in encouragement, maybe as a warning.

It didn't matter which because then my wolf caught my attention. She should be jumping for joy, begging me to let him mark my throat with a mating bite, but instead, she was glaring and pacing angrily in the corner of my mind. I froze, trying to figure out what had her so pissed off. But then I remembered the cafe. And the waitress.

I reeled back, throwing us both off balance, and we came crashing to the floor. Gabe moved fast, pulling me on top of him so he would hit the floor and break my fall. The force of the crash reverberated through the walls, yet, somehow, his hand was still on my ass.

"What was that, Ella?" he asked. His voice was thick, almost a grunt. Probably from hitting the hard floor, and it didn't help that he was still bearing my full weight. I tried to shift and take some of the pressure off him, but he refused to let me wiggle away.

"Nothing," I spat. "That was nothing. This is nothing. Let me up!"

"Ella, you're not going anywhere until we talk about what's going on with you," Gabe said. "You're running hot and cold. You can't tell me you didn't feel something just now. No one kisses like that if they don't feel something."

"No one? Not even waitresses at the cafe?"

His eyes narrowed. I took advantage of the moment and scrambled to my feet. Slowly he sat up, too.

"What waitress? Samantha?"

"I don't need to know her name," I growled. But now that I knew, I wouldn't be able to forget it. "I know what I saw, and I don't care if you have a girlfriend. Just stop messing with my head and let me leave so you can pursue…whatever you want with her."

Gabe's gaze softened, his expression of bewilderment melting into one of affection. "You're jealous of Samantha."

It was not a question. He said it as a statement. I turned red.

"Not even a little bit. I'm just grateful that you showed your true colors early on, and now I can go home. Which, by the way, is all I've wanted to do since I got here."

My voice boomed with confidence, cutting through the room like a knife. When had I gotten this bold? The regular Ella would have crawled away to lick her wounded pride alone, but here I was, confronting him face-to-face. I had to admit that it felt kind of good.

"I'm not interested in Samantha," Gabe said. He rose to his feet and tried to take me back into his arms, but I quickly moved out of reach. His arms hung limp at his side. "Samantha and I have been friends forever. I could see how it might look, though. She's always been one to push the limits of what's appropriate, and frankly, I think she does it because she knows it makes me uncomfortable."

He chuckled to himself like it was supposed to be funny. For some reason, that got under my skin even more.

"Great. So, you think it's funny for me to see you cozying up with another female werewolf? Two can play that game, Gabe," I said. I crossed my arms, trying desperately to get some of that bravado I had felt a few moments ago, but it felt impossible. As much as I hated to admit it, my feelings were hurt, and I was somehow vulnerable over this whole thing. For someone who doesn't want to mate with Gabe, what he did had way too much influence over me.

As if sensing my thoughts, Gabe moved closer again, this time boxing me in so I couldn't put the distance between us again.

"Hey," he whispered. "I'm really sorry I hurt you, Ella. It's my fault. I need to set some better boundaries with Samantha. I didn't even tell her about finding you since you were fighting our bond, but this— your jealousy, that kiss— changes everything. I know you can feel it, too.

"I'll explain to Samantha that I've found my true mate and need to change how we interact. She's a good friend. She'll understand, and I know she'll be excited to meet you."

I licked my lips, not trusting myself to respond. My wolf was listening intently but gave no indication of what she thought about Gabe's words. Human promises and interactions were sometimes more than she could truly understand. At times like this, I envied the more straightforward way she viewed the world.

"Let's just get through this mating ceremony tomorrow, and then we can discuss everything else. Okay, Gabe? We should be focused on celebrating Mariam and Trace, not arguing." There. Not a promise to reconsider, but also not something that he could really argue about. Tomorrow was a huge day for my sister; we both needed to set everything aside and be there for her.

Gabe searched my face. After getting nothing else from me, he sighed, defeated. "Yes, fine. Deal. But after that, we need to talk about this. About everything. Promise?"

I nodded, which seemed to appease him, but he didn't realize that I was crossing my fingers as I did it. This time tomorrow, I would be on a plane heading back to Dark Claw, and nothing he could say would change my mind.

I didn't bother to hide my surprise when Mariam appeared in my doorway later that night. By the time Gabe had left my room, the house was pretty quiet, and I thought everyone was asleep, trying to get enough rest for the big day tomorrow.

"What are you doing? Isn't your mate going to be upset you aren't spending the night before the ceremony with him?" I asked, setting my book down.

Mariam grinned broadly. "Nope," she said. "Apparently, Tunblewild has a tradition that mates have to be separated the night before the ceremony. Trace was going to avoid it by not telling me, but I passed Gabe in the hall, and he spilled the beans. Trace was a little pissed at him, and he promised to return the favor when you two...."

She made a dismissive motion with her hands, trailing off and sighing when she saw the look on my face. "Are you really still fighting Gabe about being true mates? You know that doesn't end well, right?"

I scooted over on the bed to make room for her, and soon she was tucked in beside me. I ran my hands through her hair, admiring the curls that she had gotten from our mother. Sharing a bed with her again made me remember those years right after Mom had died when Dad had been so lost in his own grief to know how to take care of her.

Mariam had been terribly young and looked to me as a mother substitute. It really wasn't that long ago, but here we were, ready for her mating ceremony to take place the next day.

"Goddess, Ella, are you crying?" Mariam gaped at me. I blinked, willing the unshed tears to disappear and not fall.

"No, that's stupid," I said when my voice stabilized. I nudged her with my shoulder to show her I was kidding.

"Good, because if you cry, then I'll start to cry, and then Trace will come barging in like a madman, and no one will get any sleep tonight."

I had to smile at that logic. Fair enough.

We messed with the pillows until we both found a comfortable spot. It wasn't hard, considering the size and luxury of the expensive mattress. Still, I was left staring at the ceiling long after Mariam's breathing had evened out.

"How long are you going to make him wait?" Mariam asked, startling me with the question when I thought she was fast asleep. "He loves you, you know? And he's my best friend. It hurts to see him so worried about losing you."

I wanted to tell her that asking me something like that wasn't fair. Or to point out that it was impossible for Gabe to love me as he didn't even really know me. I also considered telling her about Samantha to gauge her reaction to hearing her name, but I didn't say any of those things.

"I'm sorry you and Gabe are hurting." Those words came easily. Probably because it was the truth. I really didn't like to cause either of them so much pain and stress.

Mariam reached for my hand under the covers, and I let

her hold it. I was still widely uncomfortable with how much more physically affectionate she had become since leaving Dark Claw, but it could be a good thing. Maybe I hadn't given her enough hugs or handholds growing up, and now she was getting what she needed.

"You're doing the best you can," she whispered, almost as though she was trying to crush the doubts running wild in my head. But no, she was still talking about Gabe. I felt a little guilty knowing that I wasn't really trying to consider a future with him, but I let the emotion pass.

"We all are, Mariam," I whispered back. "We're all trying our best."

That night I had really weird dreams. They started with me being in a dark room, lying on a bed or couch, or maybe the floor because I was staring at the ceiling. Minutes drug on, turning into an hour or more. I tried tossing and turning, not of my own accord, but whoever I was in the dream. Finally, it seemed like I got comfortable enough to fall asleep, and my dream-self fell into her own sleep.

I couldn't remember anything after that, but the next morning I awoke feeling more tired than ever. Mariam was already gone, leaving behind a note about breakfast being ready whenever I decided to come down. I quickly changed out of my pajamas into a pair of leggings and a simple T-shirt. The ceremony wasn't scheduled to begin until dusk, so it didn't make sense to get dressed up before then.

I brushed my teeth and pulled my hair into a bun before setting out downstairs. I wasn't even halfway down the staircase before that fresh scent of cinnamon met my nose, and I groaned inwardly. Of course, Gabe was one of the people gathered around the kitchen table, breakfast plate and coffee in hand. I felt a little bad for him as I gave him a quick once-over. He looked as tired as I felt. I guess no one got very good sleep last night.

He zeroed in on me instantly and brought his mug to his mouth, covering the smile he gave me in greeting. I nodded at him and grabbed a plate of my own. Mariam wasn't kidding about breakfast. The catering company had set out heaping piles of fruit, meat, and biscuits for us to pick at. I grabbed a piece of fruit and some bacon, then padded over to the formal dining room. Justine smiled and gestured to the empty seat next to her at the huge table.

"How's everything going today?" I asked as I set my plate down and pulled out the chair. Randy grunted a hello. I guess he wasn't much of a morning person, either.

"Everything's great. Mariam just left for the salon. She'll take a little longer than us, what with all the honeymoon waxing and stuff." Justine raised her eyebrows suggestively, and Randy reddened, much to his mate's delight. "We should actually head over in a little bit, too. Do you want to do a dye or anything special with your hair? We could curl it or put in some nice highlights."

I shrugged. I'd never dyed my hair and usually just settled for the same old cut at Miranda's Haircuts and Shaves back in Dark Claw. She was the only stylist in the pack, so it was where pretty much everyone got their hair cut.

"Why mess with perfection?"

Gabe gave everyone at the table a cheery smile and sat in the chair across from me. I studied the fruit on my plate, trying not to engage. Of course, it didn't work, but I tried.

"So, Ella," he started. I could feel his eyes on me. "How did you sleep last night?"

I raised my eyebrows, meeting his gaze. It was a harmless question, but how he said it sounded like he already knew I didn't get much sleep. Maybe that's just how rough I looked, but I wasn't about to give him the satisfaction of confirming whatever he thought. "It was fine. No complaints."

He gave me a knowing smile like he didn't believe a word I had said. Suddenly, I wasn't very hungry anymore.

"Should we go over to the salon now? I'd like to see Mariam and maybe get a few pictures of her getting ready."

Justine nodded. "Sure. The photographer's there, too, but I can't wait to see what she looks like. I probably could use a little extra TLC, anyway."

Randy growled a warning to her. "Don't forget what we discussed. No dyes or anything shorter than your shoulders."

Justine huffed and stuck out her bottom lip. "I know, I know...nothing fun, I got it."

"Good. I need a good handful to grab onto." It was Justine's turn to blush, which was surprising. I didn't think she could get embarrassed about anything.

"That goes for you, too, Ella." Gabe's eyes were back on me. Or maybe they had never left. Either way, I frowned at him, unhappy at being told what to do.

"I haven't decided what type of style I want. I'll probably ask the cosmetologist what she thinks would look best."

"I mean it, Ella," Gabe said. Any trace of the smiling, carefree man was long gone. "I like you the way you are. A little makeup or a trim is fine, but I don't want you coming back looking different."

I snorted. "Well, that's great, but I do what I want with my body. I'll decide when I get there." I stood up, ready to bring my dishes to the sink. "Let's go, Justine. I would rather leave now if that's okay with you."

Justine looked between Gabe and me, clearly entertained by the tension building between us. I snuck a glance at him, too, expecting to see him fuming at being dismissed, but instead, he looked calm, almost thoughtful.

It was then that I decided it didn't matter what the hair stylist recommended to me. I was going to chop, dye, maybe even perm my hair to my heart's content. Maybe that would show Gabe once and for all we were not meant to be mates.

Chapter 7

She was beautiful, but that wasn't surprising. Mariam had always been gorgeous. Now, though, with her curls brushed out and her makeup done, she was a vision. I cursed myself as tears welled in my eyes again, thinking about how much I wished our parents were here. Mariam grabbed my hand, squeezing it and letting me know without words that she wanted the same thing.

I took a seat in the chair next to her. The photographer took some candid shots of us, which made me happy. These were the pictures I wanted copies of, where we were just happy and not at each other's throats. I also wanted the record to reflect that I hadn't been entirely absent during these important few days. I was here for at least some of it.

"What do you want to have done?" The stylist untied my messy bun, and my hair cascaded down my back, resting on the black cape she had secured around me.

Did I dare?

I caught a glimpse of myself in the mirror. I was the same old Ella with the same old dull look. I needed something new, and this was as good a time as any to break out of my rut. Sending a message to Gabe that I wasn't his to boss around would just be a bonus.

———————

"Seriously. Are you a masochist or something?" Justine asked, eyeing the color in my hair with envy. The stylist had just finished blow-drying it, and the purple was coming through nicely. I grinned at my reflection, enjoying the difference already. "I know you said you wanted a mate who would discipline you, and if this sort of thing is typical, I don't think that will be an issue."

"You said *what*?" Mariam was sitting on a nearby sofa, flipping through a magazine and waiting for her wax. We had her full attention now, though.

I blushed. "I didn't say I wanted to be punished. I said I wanted a strong mate, not someone like Gabe. He's just so polite and friendly…which is great, but I want what you both have. I want sparks and passion."

I waited for them to argue with me and tell me that Gabe could be a strong mate for me, but they didn't. For some reason, my heart sank slightly, knowing that they must agree.

True to her word, Justine got a trim and left her flaming red hair its natural color. To be honest, I'm not sure any dye would have taken, anyway. Her hair seemed bent on remaining the color of fire.

"I'm starving, and I'm guessing you are, too, since you barely ate anything at breakfast," Justine said to me. "Let's grab something from the diner before going back and stepping into the chaos."

Mariam readily agreed, but I hesitated. *It could be a totally different diner, right?* But as soon as we started walking toward Town Hall, I knew exactly where we were going. Still, that didn't mean Gabe's friend—Samantha—would be working there.

But she was. Of course, she was.

"Hey Samantha, what's the special today?" Mariam asked as we sat in a big booth by the window. It was so close to where Gabe had been sitting, I could almost reach out and touch him if he was there now.

"We've got a French dip with macaroni salad or lasagna with garlic bread," Samantha answered, grabbing her notepad, and clicking the end of her pen. "Who's this?"

She looked me over, not bothering to hide her curiosity. I glanced at her but didn't dare scrutinize her in the same way. Samantha gave off a decidedly confident vibe, and I deflated a little, for some reason thinking about how I couldn't measure up against her.

"This is my sister, Ella. She's here visiting for the mating ceremony," Mariam explained.

"And she's Gabe's *true mate*," blurted Justine. Mariam must have kicked her from under the table because she punctuated her statement with an "oof."

Samantha's eyes widened with surprise. There was another emotion there, too. Whatever she was feeling, it looked painful. But she quickly recovered and shrugged her shoulder like it didn't matter.

"Oh yeah? Well, good for him," she said. "So, what do you three want to eat?"

Justine and Mariam both ordered the French dip. I nodded to get the same thing, not caring what I ate. I watched as Samantha walked back toward the kitchen, her movements stiff and awkward, like she was trying to play it cool but failing.

I knew that walk well, myself.

"Where's the bathroom?" I asked.

Mariam gestured toward the same hallway Samantha went down. I nodded and stood, wanting to move fast before I lost my nerve. I walked around the wall that blocked the area from the view of the diners but ignored the restroom and continued toward the kitchen.

Sitting on an overturned bucket was Samantha. She was crying.

This was a bad idea. I turned to leave, but it was too late.

"Ella? Did you need something?" Samantha asked, sniffling, and trying to hide her tears.

"I'm really sorry," I said, jumping straight into an apology. "I wanted to talk to you, but this is a bad time. I'll see you around. And I hope you feel better."

"Wait. I'm sorry, Ella. I know Gabe is your true mate and everything. It's just…."

Samantha trailed off, not finishing the sentence, but her thoughts were clear enough. If I was my sister, I'd probably pull her in for a hug or something, but I'm not, so I just stood there wringing my hands.

"Was it serious between you?" I asked. Samantha's eyes widened, and I cringed. "I don't mean it like that. Not in a jealous way. In fact, we probably won't even end up together. I saw the two of you the other day, I mean. Here, at the cafe. Gabe said nothing was going on between you, but clearly, that's not the case."

"You think Gabe and I…." Her eyes were puffy from all the crying, but now they were more hopeful than anything.

"I mean, you wouldn't mind if Gabe and I became chosen mates? You would be fine with that?"

My throat went dry. My wolf whined under her breath. She understood that the female in front of us wanted our mate, and I waited for the intense feelings of possessiveness to pour from her, but nothing came. My own heart was beating in overtime. Was I really okay with that?

Samantha started grinning, her face lighting up as she took my silence as a yes. "Oh my gosh, thank you, Ella. I can't wait to tell Gabe."

I gave her a wobbly smile and left her to go back to the table. Sure, losing a true mate to someone else would probably be a little sad for anyone, but this was for the best. At least, that is what I told myself as I stuffed my feelings, and my wolf's feelings, down deep inside.

"You're being really quiet. Is everything okay?"

We were headed back to the alpha house after lunch. I glanced at Mariam in the driver's seat. She was right; I knew I had barely spoken a word while she and Justine had gushed about the mating vacation Trace was taking her on. It was somewhere in Europe, fancy and romantic, but I couldn't focus on what was being said. My thoughts were still on Samantha and what happened in the kitchen.

"Of course," I said, perking up. "Can you believe the big night is tonight? We've only got another few hours before the ceremony. Do you want to start getting ready right away, or are there last-minute things to take care of first?"

Mariam shook her head, a small smile on her lips. "Uh-

uh. I know you, Ella. Thanks for being all in for me, but whatever's bothering you is big. Did something happen at the diner? Everything was going great with your awesome new hair, but when you came back from the bathroom, it was like you had deflated or something."

You should tell her about the female at the diner, my wolf prodded. *She knows her and our mate. Maybe she can help.*

I chewed on my lip. I wasn't sure if I wanted Mariam to help, even if she could. The more I thought about the Gabe/Samantha thing, the more it made sense. I wasn't going to wreck their happiness just so I could be with a man I wasn't even sure I wanted. Gabe was too honorable to ask if he could be with the waitress instead, but now he wouldn't have to. They could carry on like they had before.

"It's nothing. Just getting kind of sentimental, you know?"

"Really? You, sentimental?" Mariam scrunched up her face as she put the car in park. "I'm not buying it, Els. To be continued, for sure."

I sighed and opened the car door. The smell of cinnamon was still hanging around on the breeze, so I knew Gabe must be nearby. I ran a hand self-consciously through my hair. Until Mariam had mentioned it, I had almost completely forgotten about the makeover and Gabe's list of demands that I had thrown out the window. I had done it to make a statement, but maybe it wouldn't even be necessary now.

"Better face the music," Mariam murmured, glancing at my hand still tucked into my purple hair. Justine parked next to Mariam, and the three of us walked to the door together. Randy was waiting for us in the foyer.

"I'm proud of you for listening, troublemaker. Beautiful as always," he said, scooping Justine into his arms. He was trying not to be obvious, but I could tell he was glancing at me and likely thanking the Goddess I wasn't his responsibility.

I snuck a peek around Randy and locked eyes with Gabe. His eyes flashed, darkening in a way that I hadn't expected. Where was the boy I thought might still be in his late teens? It was like he had disappeared entirely.

"Would you all excuse us? Ella and I need a few moments alone."

I gulped. Even knowing that nothing would come from the time we spent together, the instant worry was like a reflex. Something in his tone sent alarm bells ringing in my head.

"Are you going to be alright?" Mariam whispered. "Do you need me to come with you?"

I shook my head and did my best to put on a mask of indifference. What I needed to tell him would be easier without an audience, anyway. Shrugging, I walked past Gabe and straight up the stairs to my room. He followed closely, with his hand on my hip.

Gabe quietly closed the door behind us before descending upon me. Although his features were relaxed, his canines had started growing, and he had to blink a few times to keep the wolf from showing in his eyes.

"Do you enjoy disobeying me, Ella?" His words were smooth, almost like a purr. He took a few steps closer. My wolf was whimpering, ready to show her belly in submission. "I don't think my instructions were hard to understand. You were told to only get a trim, but is that what you did?"

"N-no," I stammered. Gabe smiled, the look of a predator flashing across his face.

"Mariam and Justine both have a wild streak, but I thought you would have been the voice of reason. Instead, you were the only one who refused to listen to the rules you were given. I'll have to ensure you understand what happens if you disobey me, mate."

I scowled at him. "Gabe, we haven't agreed to be mates. I have no reason to obey you. Besides, I don't think you have it in you to discipline anyone for anything. Can we just move on? I need to tell you what happened today at lunch and—"

"And I'd love to hear all about it, really, but first, we need to take care of your disobedience." Gabe sat on the bed and patted his lap. It took a moment for me to realize what he was doing, but when I could feel the color drain from my face.

"You don't mean you want me to…you know?" I couldn't even bring myself to say it.

"I absolutely expect my mate to face the consequences of her actions, and the consequences of your actions today include taking a trip over my knee," Gabe answered. His words were tight and clipped, but at least he didn't look as intimidating as when he first saw my hair in the foyer. Maybe I could talk him out of this madness.

"Gabe—" I started.

"Gabe, nothing," he snapped. "You did what you wanted, despite what I told you to do, so now you can make up for it by being a good she-wolf and laying your lovely ass across my lap."

So much for talking him out of the madness. The way his jaw was set told me there was no negotiating on this. Maybe if I could just get through it and then explain about Samantha, we wouldn't ever have to see each other again. I set my own mask back in place and walked up to him, spreading myself over his lap. I tried to think about the book I was reading or the mating ceremony, anything but the way he smelled or the heat coming off his body. Against my will, wetness pooled between my legs.

He chuckled above me, amused about something. I risked a look back at him, which seemed to set his gaze on fire.

"When you look at me like that, Ella, over your shoulder with your ass perched on me, it gives me all sorts of ideas," he rumbled. "But you seem to be confused about how this works. As your mate, when I have to discipline you, it will be on your bare skin, not through a thick pair of pants."

I gaped at him. "These aren't thick! They're leggings, Gabe. There's practically nothing there at all. I'm not taking them off. Now, can we just get this over with so I can tell you what happened?"

"Not a chance," he spat. "And arguing after disobeying isn't a great look, Ella. Take off the pants and the underwear so I can punish you, then I'll hear about the rest of your day."

My wolf willed me to obey him, and his words were oddly challenging to ignore, but I refused to back down. I mumbled under my breath, praying it was enough to end this foolishness.

"What? I can't hear you."

"I said I'm not wearing underwear," I blurted, probably

loud enough for the rest of the house to hear. My face burned, and I hid it in the bedding. "Leggings show panty lines, and so I just skipped them."

Gabe froze and then ran his hand gently over my butt. I wiggled, wanting to break away but also getting wetter by the second. "I bet that's why I can scent your arousal so much clearer today," he said in a strangled voice. "Take them off, Ella."

His voice was so firm, and insistent. My wolf begged me to listen. Slowly, I stood and reached for the waistband of the leggings. I hesitated, not wanting to give him a show in the process. I turned to the side so my sex was obstructed and pulled them off with one fluid motion. Without a word, I settled back on his lap, though I could feel his hardness through his jeans this time. I squirmed against it, trying to get comfortable.

"Goddess, Ella," Gabe moaned. "If you keep that up, you'll get more than just a punishment out of this."

I froze. I had been around plenty of naked men in my life. That was part of being a shifter, having to see other people nude occasionally. But I had never looked at their genitals. Besides basic mechanics, I had no idea really what to expect from the physical side of being mated.

If the bulge in Gabe's jeans was any indication, I'm pretty sure it wouldn't even fit inside of me. Not that I was going to try.

Gabe took a shaky breath and rested his hand on my backside, this time directly on my skin. "I'm going to give you ten with my hand, okay? I want you to count for me."

I was thinking about arguing when the first one landed. I cried out, wanting it to stop already.

"Count, Ella," Gabe reminded me.

"One," I said miserably. How was I going to make it to ten?

Whap. "Two!" I hollered.

It went on like that all the way to ten. I called out the last number in between sobs. Gabe started massaging my cheeks, and I was too upset to feel embarrassed, so I let him.

"Shhhh," he said, pulling me into his arms. "It's all done, Ella. You did great. And I think you'll remember this the next time you want to disobey."

The next time? That was enough to break off my tears and had me up searching for my pants. Gabe reached for me and let his arm drop when I made no attempt to return to him.

"This is important for us, Ella," he said. "Let me comfort you and remind you that I love you."

"What? What did you say?" I asked, blinking. Clearly, I had misheard him.

Gabe frowned. "Aftercare is important. Your punishment was warranted, but things between us will always return to normal afterward. The punishment acts like a reset. Don't you want to cuddle or...aren't you, you know?"

I stared at him blankly.

"Aren't you turned on, too?" His cheeks were red.

The truth was I was turned on. He could probably tell that, too, if his nostrils flaring were any indication. But all that didn't matter. Gabe had just told me he loves me, despite having an attachment to Samantha.

"I went to the diner today," I said evenly. I pulled up the

leggings, refusing to have this conversation naked. "I went with Mariam and Justine after the hair appointment. Samantha was there."

"Okay," he said slowly. "How is she? I would have taken you to meet her, you know. I just haven't had a chance."

I snorted. "I'm sure that would've been a million times more awkward, so I'm glad you weren't there. Just know that everything is fine. I'm fine with it, really. None of this changes anything."

I gestured to Gabe and myself, hoping he'd take the hint and not make me say out loud that being bare-butt naked and having him spank and caress my body wouldn't come between him and the other female.

Thankfully, he nodded. "I agree. This doesn't change anything. That's what I was trying to say, anyway."

"Okay, then. I need to change and find Mariam, so if you wouldn't mind...." I nodded to the door, and he seemed to get the hint, though he looked bewildered.

"You're really not mad? Everything between us is okay?"

"Yes," I said, exasperated. "And it doesn't have to be weird for you and Mariam, either. I mean, you two can still be friends."

This earned me a laugh, which felt like a knife twisting in my gut. "Okay, I'm glad to hear that, too. I'll see you in a little while, Ella."

I closed the door, not trusting myself to answer. For some unknown reason, I was on the verge of tears.

Chapter 8

Gabe ran his fingers over the collar of the new shirt, pulling the stiff fabric away from his skin. He was used to wearing suits every day in the office, but he usually had the good sense to have them cleaned before putting them on for the first time. The problem was now his mind and routines felt completely frazzled. He didn't know which way was up, and he didn't really care. Everything revolved around Ella and making her realize they were meant to be together.

He smiled into the mirror, liking how the shirt cut across his chest. Too often, Gabe was a little self-conscious about his lean figure. Comparing himself to Randy and Trace always made him wish he was born with the same brute muscle they had. Gabe cringed, thinking about how Ella had mistaken him for a teenager when they first met. He could have gone his whole life without being reminded by her that he had a little bit of a baby face.

She doesn't think that anymore. Gabe's wolf grinned, content to roll on his back and relive this morning's events. It was impossible to prevent those images from running through his mind, too. Ella, with her perfect ass across his lap, her bright eyes filled with tears and the scent of her arousal thick in the air. Gabe had wanted to run his fingers up her thigh and feel how wet she was for him, but he needed to remain firm in her punishment.

He adjusted himself at the mere thought of going further with her. It was enough to make him rock hard again.

What's more, she seemed to be accepting their bond for the first time. Before shooing him out, she said something about being fine with everything and how it wouldn't change anything between them. Well, of course, punishing her wouldn't change anything between them. He frowned, wondering why she even thought that it would. All male werewolves had to discipline their mates at some point. It was an honor and a responsibility that he took very seriously.

Gabe flexed his hand, still slightly sore from her spanking. He looked forward to showing her precisely what kind of mate he'd be.

"You almost ready?" The voice on the other side of the bathroom door rumbled like chewed-up gravel. Randy was there when he opened it, messing with the buttons on his shirt. "I hate these things," he complained.

Gabe laughed. "Let's go. The ceremony's about to start." He paused, looking behind him. "Where's Justine?"

"She's helping Mariam." Randy shook his head. "Jess decided last minute to stay home and not attend the ceremony. Something about… well, you know."

Gabe did know, but he was still a little surprised. At one time, Jess had hoped to be Trace's chosen mate, but after she acknowledged that he was settling down with Mariam, the three of them became really good friends. He knew that Samantha had expected them to be together at one point, and their story gave Gabe hope that they could still be close after he mated with Ella. "You don't mean she still has a thing for Trace? That feels so long ago. Is Mariam alright?"

"Don't know, but I'm sure it's fine. Just don't say anything about it to Trace. He doesn't need to worry about Jess's feelings at his mating ceremony," Randy said.

Gabe nodded. He grabbed his phone and wallet off the counter and followed Randy to the backyard. Members of the pack were already showing up, and they were finding a place to sit on the pillows strewn across the lawn. Gabe loved mating ceremonies for what they were: a chance to celebrate two shifters committing to each other for life. But all the trapping and decorations weren't really his thing. He looked over everything without much interest. That is until he saw Ella standing at the front, waiting for someone.

Waiting for me, he thought.

As much as he hated her disobedience at the salon, Gabe couldn't deny that her haircut and dye complimented her natural beauty. Some people might find it a surprising choice since Ella was so quiet a lot of the time, but he knew there was more to her than just a few shy smiles and faraway looks. His mate was deep and complex. She was fun, just like her new hair.

Her dress fit her perfectly, too. He didn't have the same moment of pride as when she wore the black one he selected for her, but this one showed off her flawless figure perfectly. It was also modest, which he knew was important to her. Gabe had to grin, knowing he was the only one who knew exactly what she looked like underneath the yards of fabric.

"Aren't you going to sit with Samantha?" she asked, her eyes widening as she took in Gabe's formal wear. His smile deepened, realizing he could have the same effect on her that she had on him. That is, until her words hit home.

"Why would I be sitting with Samantha?" he asked incredulously. Gabe didn't even know where Samantha was. Probably somewhere in the crowd, but there were easily two thousand shifters on the lawn, and none of them called to him the way Ella did. They might as well be a sea of strangers.

She was about to answer, but her alpha, Jeremy, began addressing everyone instead.

"Thank you all for coming this evening," he boomed over the talking crowd. The sound of his alpha voice was enough to cause a ripple of silence that spread over the entire backyard. "It is my pleasure to perform this mating ceremony. I know it is a very important event for the Tumblewild pack, but it is also a special day for Dark Claw and the bridge being made between our two communities."

Most pack members nodded, though there were a few scoffs, too. No one had forgotten about the wild goose chase Trace had to go on to secure Mariam as his mate, and more than a few members blamed Jeremy for not having better control over Mariam when she was a member of his pack.

Of course, the one who knew her well didn't find any fault in Jeremy. Mariam wasn't about to do a damn thing she didn't want to, and it was one of the things everyone loved about her. Personally, Gabe thought that the pack's judgment against her was unfair, anyway. Expecting all female shifters to fall in line just because their alpha wanted something was unrealistic. Their mates, on the other hand, had a lot more ammunition to work with. He slid his gaze back to Ella, imagining how convincing he would be with her writhing beneath him.

Ella wasn't paying attention to him, though. Her eyes were jumping between Mariam and someone in the crowd. Frowning, Gabe followed her line of sight and spotted Samantha standing off to the side. He smiled at her, and she gave him a small wave in return.

Jeremy was going over pack law and tradition, leading up to the couple expressing their desire to be mated. Randy grabbed Justine's hand as Trace said his vows. Gabe's palm itched. He wanted to place his hand in Ella's, and why shouldn't he?

Before he could talk himself out of it, Gabe grasped his mate's hand. She looked at him, startled, then confused. Her attention turned back to Samantha, but at least she didn't try to pull away.

Justine gave the same moving speech about growing up as Trace's sister that we heard yesterday, and then all eyes turned to Ella, waiting for her to say a few words about Mariam. Ella cleared her throat, shaking slightly.

"Since our parents died, it was always just Mariam and me against the world," she said. "I was the older sister, always trying to put her on the right path, and you, Mare, were the younger sister, trying to get away with everything. Some things never change, but I'm sure Trace will be a better enforcer of rules than I was."

"Here, here," Trace agreed. Laughter filled the space.

"Mariam, since you've met Trace, you've changed into someone even more amazing than you were before. I know you never really looked up to me, but I want you to know I look up to you. Hopefully, I'll find the same happiness you have one day."

Mariam glanced at Gabe, communicating exactly what he was thinking. *One day she'll find that kind of happiness? What about right now?*

It was like having the breath knocked out of him. What could she have meant by that? Gabe was so consumed with his thoughts that the rest of the ceremony passed in a blur.

"I'm happy to introduce the newly mated alpha couple, Mr. and Mrs. Everett," Jeremy said at last. "I hope you will all join them in a Tumblewild pack run."

And that was that. The ceremony was, by most accounts, over. Mariam and Trace exited the stage and disappeared into one of the many changing tents that had been set up. When they emerged, both had already shifted, prompting others in the audience to walk toward the other changing rooms or just begin disrobing where they stood.

Not a pack member himself, Jeremy followed tradition and excused himself from the stage, likely to eat some of the delicious-smelling food or return to wherever he was staying in town.

Gabe turned to reach for Ella's hand again, but she was following Jeremy. She didn't even look back to where he was standing. He wanted to follow her and clear things up between them. He definitely wanted to ask her what the hell she meant about finding happiness one day, but suddenly Samantha was in his way.

"Hey, Gabe," she said, blocking his view of Ella. "You're going to shift and join the run, right? Do you want to run together?"

"I need to speak with Ella," Gabe said, moving to go around her, but she caught his arm.

"I spoke with Ella earlier," said Samantha. "She said she didn't have a problem with it. With any of it, Gabe. We can be together, and she'll be happy for us."

He blinked a few times, confused. "Samantha, we've been over this. We're just friends. That's it. You know I'm only interested in finding my true mate, and now she's here."

"Really?" Samantha huffed. "If she's really your true mate, why is she fine with you being with me? Her wolf would have prevented her from offering us a chance to be together. Clearly, she doesn't feel the same way you do."

Gabe's heart sank at the possibility. If what Samantha said was true, Ella must not think he was her true mate. It was one more thing they'd need to get settled.

Samantha's eyes shifted to something over Gabe's shoulder, causing him to turn around. Ella was watching them. She was talking to Jeremy, but every few seconds she slyly looked their way. A slow smile crossed Samantha's face when Gabe turned back to her.

"I've wanted to do this for a long time," she said. She stood on her tiptoes and threw her arms around Gabe's shoulders. Her lips pressed against his, hot and needy. He was momentarily stunned but withdrew with a scowl as soon as he registered what was happening.

"What the hell, Samantha?" he growled. His wolf was

going nuts and close to forcing a shift. The animal pushed to the front, showing in Gabe's eyes, and talking through him in a deep voice. "You're not to touch us, female."

His words were so sharp that Samantha visibly flinched. The whole exchange had drawn more than a few curious looks, and she blushed up to the roots of her hair. Samantha ducked away, likely embarrassed by the forcefulness of his rejection. Gabe's heart hurt for her, but she had no right to force herself on him like that. It was unacceptable.

Our mate is gone. His wolf had tucked himself back inside Gabe's body, but the urgency of his words said he was ready to shift if he gave consent. The wolf was right; Ella and Jeremy were both missing.

Behind Gabe, the alpha pair howled their invitation for everyone to join in on the pack run. All around him, shifted werewolves answered and joined the couple. Gabe felt his wolf prodding him to shift and follow. The alpha call was too much to resist when given within earshot. If he didn't comply, the beast inside him would override the decision and force the shift anyway.

Against his will and better judgment, Gabe removed his clothing and shifted, joining the other wolves in celebrating the mating of their alpha.

The run was exhilarating, but Gabe couldn't focus on the happiness in the air or the sweet-smelling dirt beneath his paws. He couldn't shake the sight of Ella standing with Jeremy, watching as Samantha took advantage of him. He wanted to know what they were talking about and where they went. He wanted to explain the unwanted kiss, which made him angry enough to push his wolf to run even faster. What had Samantha been playing at by doing that?

Finally, several hours later, the run began to wind down. The mated pair led the pack back up the hill toward the alpha house. Gabe usually tried to shift in one of the changing rooms, but he didn't really care about modesty at the moment. He just wanted to find Ella as quickly as possible.

Once his clothes were hastily thrown back on, Gabe raced to the alpha house and flung the door wide open. Something was wrong; the air inside felt quiet. Too quiet.

Her smell, like flowers and sunshine, was still there, but he knew she was gone. But that didn't stop him from running around and checking all the room anyway.

When he opened the door to her bedroom, Ella's bags and her book on the nightstand were gone. Instead, two notes sat on the bedspread. One was for Mariam, and he set it back down without reading it. The other was addressed to him.

Gabe,

I'm going back home with Jeremy. He thinks he may have found a good chosen mate for me. I'm sure we'll see each other again when I visit Mariam sometime, and I hope you find all the happiness in the world with Samantha. She seems really nice.

Please don't think you have to contact me. I'm not changing my mind.

Best wishes,

Ella

Gabe reread the note a few times, trying to make it make sense. Ella was gone. She was rejecting their mating bond to go and mate with another male, which put both him and his wolf on edge.

The female is ours, the wolf roared. *Who else could have a claim to her?*

The letter didn't say.

He slowly sank onto the bed, unsure of what to do. Should he go and try to find her? Should he bring her back to Tumblewild against her will and claim her, as was his right?

Gabe frowned. That's what Randy, Trace, and just about any other werewolf would do in this situation. But he wasn't them. He wanted Ella to come to him freely. He didn't want to chase her down and force her to choose him. That wouldn't be any kind of choice at all.

His thoughts started spiraling. What if she breaks the bond by mating with another male, only to realize her mistake afterward? What if the asshole who mates with her is abusive or crazy? What if he's perfect for her, and Gabe wasn't her true mate after all?

The different scenarios and what-ifs kept coming, weighing him down and making him even more unsure of what to do.

Letting out a slow breath, Gabe made a decision. He would be here for Ella the moment she decided to return, but he wouldn't follow her and try to make her see reason. He had to trust that the goddess knew what she was doing by tying them together.

That was about all he could do.

Chapter 9

"What makes you so sure about this?" Jeremy asked. "Is it that you just want to stay in Dark Claw?"

I nodded, thanking him for giving me an easy out. The truth was that I didn't really care that much about staying with my pack. I would miss the bakery, and part of me didn't want to leave the home I had grown up in with my parents and, later, with Mariam. But more than anything, I just wanted to distance myself from Gabe and put everything that happened in Tumblewild behind me.

"Who did you have in mind? You said someone in Dark Claw might be interested in being chosen mates with me?"

Jeremy nodded slowly, carefully, like he was trying to think of how to best say what he was thinking. That couldn't be good. The pause was heavy as he maneuvered his rental car into the airport parking garage. The rental company was located next to the parking garage, making the return quick so we could easily catch the flight home.

"Have you ever met Neil?" he asked finally.

"I don't think we've ever spoken to each other, but I know who he is, of course. That's not who you're thinking of, though, right? Wouldn't he be more interested in a beta female type? Maybe someone from another pack?"

I chewed on my lip nervously. The sooner I was mated to someone else, the sooner the thought of Gabe wouldn't make me want to run back to Tumblewild. Mariam disliked Neil for whatever reason, but I knew beggars couldn't be choosers.

I knew I was leaving just in time, too. Being close to Gabe and watching him kiss Samantha was too much for me to take. My wolf had almost taken her head off when she was pressed against our mate.

He won't be our mate for long, I reminded her. *I'll find someone for you who will be a better fit.*

She gave me an irritated snort, and I had to agree that the promise sounded hollow. But even if we wanted Gabe, he was clearly entangled with someone else. Maybe he would mate with Samantha right away, and I wouldn't have to mate with Neil or anyone. I sat up a little straighter at the thought; only one of us had to find a chosen mate for our bond to break. Maybe I could afford to take this slow if he didn't.

It took me a minute to realize Jeremy had said something and was now looking at me, waiting for a response. "Sorry, what did you say?"

He sighed. "I asked if you would be interested in Neil courting you? You know…maybe getting to know each other a little bit to see if you're compatible."

Dating. Jeremy meant dating, but that was kind of a taboo thing in our pack. Dating said you were going against waiting for your true mate, and it seemed to encourage promiscuity, so most of Dark Claw called it courting. Whatever it was, it wasn't exactly encouraged.

"Yeah, I'd be open to that," I said. Maybe having a chosen mate wouldn't be so bad after all.

Jeremy bought me a ticket back home, even though I offered to pay for the high-priced, last-minute flight myself. We never really had any reason to interact beyond him complaining to me about Mariam's behavior and then trying to find her when she went rogue, but he seemed like a nice enough person. He was tired, more than anything. Being an alpha was taking a toll on him. Trace appeared to handle the stress much better, and I had to wonder if that was because he had an excellent beta couple in Justine and Randy or if it was because Mariam helped take some of the load off of him. Or maybe he was just better at being an alpha, period.

Jeremy spent most of the flight asleep or checking his emails, so the conversation between us died until we touched down in California. It was just as well. I was tempted to ask him about his own plans for finding a mate, but that was probably inappropriate. The last thing I needed was for Jeremy to think I was interested in courting him, too.

"I need to head over to one of the human city council meetings, but I'll get you a cab back to Dark Claw," he said quietly when we were far enough away from the other passengers so that they wouldn't overhear. He seemed like he wanted to say something else but wasn't sure how to. I stared at him, waiting.

"I'll talk to Neil if you're sure that's what you want," he offered, giving me an unreadable look.

I nodded. "Yeah, it's for the best."

He looked thoughtful but didn't answer. Instead, he

hailed a cab, paid the driver, and shut the door behind me. With a small wave, he blended into the crowd, and I tugged my seatbelt into place.

The cab driver was playing some soft jazz, and it was soothing. I allowed my mind to drift back to the look on my alpha's face when he asked for the hundredth time if I was sure about leaving Gabe for good. I couldn't understand why he was so hesitant on my behalf. After all, he had seen Samantha and Gabe making out at the mating ceremony, too. Obviously, the goddess had made a mistake pairing us together.

The bakery looked the same, at least from the outside when I drove by it. It had long since closed for the night, as it was almost one in the morning. The house was definitely the same. Everything was the same, really. But then, it had only been a few days since I had left for Tumblewild. I wasn't really sure what I was expecting. Maybe for everything to look as different as I felt inside.

I lugged my bag into the back bedroom and began to unpack. The unpacking was the worst part of any trip, but this time I didn't mind it. It was a mindless task, and I enjoyed turning my brain off to do it. The toothbrush goes back into the bathroom, pajamas go into the washing machine. Easy stuff.

Only when everything was set right, and I made myself a cup of tea did I notice and hate how quiet the house was. I was used to being home alone. Mariam often didn't spend the night at the house during the last few years she technically lived here. I found out later she had spent most of those nights at her boyfriend Patrick's apartment, but I never minded the quiet then. It was peaceful, and usually,

I'm peaceful, too, so it worked out well. But now, the silence was driving me nuts.

My wolf whined that we should go to our mate and beg him to take us back.

He knows where we are if he really wants to be with us, I chided her. That was a half-truth. He knew I was back home, but I had written in the letter that he shouldn't come after me. It was a last-minute addition, written as a PS, and even now, I wasn't sure why I had felt compelled to include it. Maybe just to try to prevent him from feeling obligated to pursue me.

Maybe because I wouldn't have been strong enough to tell him to his face to leave me alone.

I felt a little antsy, and I knew why. Female werewolves were driven to be close to their mates, and I had left mine in another state. To be fair, Gabe was probably going through something much worse. Distance between mates could drive a male werewolf crazy, at least until the relationship was consummated. I shuddered, recalling how incensed Trace had been when Mariam had left him.

But Gabe wasn't Trace. He wasn't an intense, dominant mate, so who knows what he felt. And unlike Trace, all he had to do was mate with Samantha, and all those feelings would disappear.

I fell into a restless sleep, frowning and wondering why he hadn't just done it already.

———

"You seem tired," Heather said. She rearranged the fruit tarts on a tray for the display case while I started a fresh pot of coffee.

"It's four in the morning," I answered. That should be a good enough reason to be tired, but usually I was awake and ready for my shift at the bakery without so much as a yawn. Today felt like I was moving in slow motion, and I was struggling to keep my eyes open.

Heather gave me a look like she wasn't buying it. We had been opening the bakery together for years, and she knew I was naturally an early riser. Working in a bakery was perfect for me, given the hours.

"It's not just that," she said. "You've been distracted today. How was the mating ceremony? What was it like in Tumblewild?"

Like most female shifters, Heather had never been to another pack. Unlike males who sometimes went searching for their true mate, females didn't really have a reason to leave home unless there was some family event, like Mariam's ceremony.

"It was alright," I said carefully. Heather stood, waiting for me to say more. I sighed. "Fine. I met my true mate there, but it doesn't matter because he's in love with someone else. It's fine. We weren't a good match, anyway."

"What?!" Heather dropped a tart on the floor. "You mean to tell me that you found your true mate, and you're going to let him get away? Just like that?"

I scowled. "Not just like that. I told you. Gabe already has a girlfriend, and he seemed… well, he seemed like he wouldn't be able to give me what I need from a mate."

"Let me get this straight: you, Ella, who has been waiting for your true mate for almost 40 years, found him, only to let some girlfriend get in the way? Have you lost your mind?"

"It's more than just that," I said, though when she put it like that, it did sound stupid. "He's not... tough. He doesn't have a strong backbone, and he's not bossy. He's... different."

"So are you," Heather pointed out. "Look, I don't know what you mean by 'won't give you whatever,' but you're too smart to let a true mate go. If you give it a try, it will probably work out. It's meant to be, like they say."

I didn't want to argue anymore, so I just shrugged and nodded.

For the rest of my shift, Heather kept throwing me exasperated looks, but I pretended that I didn't see them, and we didn't discuss the topic of true mates again. The bakery was thankfully busy, otherwise I probably would have gotten another earful from her. I was just clocking out and taking off my apron when my phone buzzed with another incoming text. There were already several that I had left unanswered.

Mariam: Just tell me one thing. Why????

I sighed and put it back in my pocket. I wasn't in the mood for another lecture, and she should be focusing on her post-ceremony vacation anyway. Trace would probably take her cell from her at some point if she didn't stop texting me. My phone buzzed again, and I pulled it back out, this time to just turn the stupid thing off, but I stopped when I noticed it wasn't from my sister.

Unknown: Jeremy gave me your number. Dinner tonight?

I frowned for a moment before remembering that Jeremy was setting me up with Neil. I hesitated, not sure how to respond. I had agreed to go out with him, but this felt too soon. I hated being rushed.

Me: Hey Neil. Thanks for the message. I just got back into town yesterday. I'm going to take a few days to just relax before jumping into anything new. Would a day next week work for you?

I hit send and waited. I tidied the back shelves and rotated the stock, thinking he might suggest another day to meet up. A few minutes turned into a half hour, but when I checked my notifications again, there was still no response. Not a big deal; he was the beta, and something probably came up. I pocketed my phone and headed to my car. I put the key in the ignition and frowned when it sputtered but wouldn't turn over. It was an old Toyota that my mom used to drive before she passed away years early. The car was at least twenty-five years old but had never given me any major problems before.

I tried a few more times, but it wouldn't turn over. I prayed that it was just the starter and not something more serious. Either way, it looked like I'd need a tow and someone to drive me home.

Rotten luck, that's what this was. And I was not in the mood for anything else to go wrong.

I looked around, praying that Heather was still nearby, but her car was gone. Usually, I'd call Mariam, but that wasn't an option anymore, either. I tried her friend Patrick since he worked at the auto garage, but he wasn't answering.

I sighed, slumping against the seat. I might have to leave the car where it was until someone with a tow truck could pick it up. But there were only a few Lyft drivers in the pack and no real taxis. Abandoning the car would probably mean walking all the way back home.

Movement in the rearview mirror caught my attention. It was someone pulling up behind me. The dark color and size of the vehicle made it foreboding and a little familiar. Frowning, I tried to remember where I had seen the big, black truck before. I didn't have to wonder for long. The driver stepped out and gave a charming, lopsided smile. It was Neil driving the same truck that helped him and Jeremy search for Mariam.

My wolf prickled at the way he looked me over from where I sat. I had to admit that it made me uncomfortable, too. I rolled down the window as he approached the driver's side.

"Hey, Ella. Everything okay?" The question sounded innocent enough, but it felt weird for him to ask. For all he knew, I was just sitting in my car after a long shift. Unless he heard my engine sputtering, I guess.

"Not really," I admitted. "My car won't start, and Patrick isn't answering."

"Patrick?" The name soured in his throat. "Why are you calling him?"

"He works in the auto-body shop," I pointed out. "And I have his number because he and Mariam used to be… close."

Neil smirked, but the smile didn't reach his eyes. "You should lose his number. Let me give you a ride home, and then I can sort out your car."

I hesitated. What he said made sense. It was a nice thing to do, offering to help me out, but how he said it didn't sound like an offer. It sounded like an order.

"Okay," I said slowly, rolling the window back up and

opening the door to join him on the sidewalk. I shrugged my purse onto my shoulder and followed him to the truck. "Thanks for stopping."

"It was good timing," he said smoothly, opening my passenger door. "I'm happy to help."

He could be more help by just leaving us alone, my wolf argued. *I could get us home fast.*

Clearly, she wasn't a fan, and she had a point. Shifting and running home would have been another good option. It was too late to back out now, though. I clipped my seatbelt on, noticing Neil's remained unfastened.

"You have to turn left at the light," I prompted. His laugh was like a bark, and it sent a chill up my spine.

"I know where you live, Ella. I'm the pack's beta, remember?"

Of course, he knew my address. How could I forget? He'd been there several times over the past few months because of Mariam. My cheeks went pink over the mistake.

"You're cute when you're embarrassed," he said, reaching over to caress the blush on my face. I jerked away, not expecting the sudden contact. His hand fell without protest, but the smile was gone from his face.

I wasn't sure how to respond, so we drove for a while in silence. I was hoping he would apologize for trying to touch me, and I'd tell him it was no big deal, and we could move on to another topic, but that never happened. It was Neil who eventually broke it.

"So, what made you do that to your hair?"

I almost laughed, but a glance in his direction told me he was serious. "It's just hair, Neil. I wanted a change, so I made one. I like it."

"Don't get me wrong. It doesn't look bad. It's just not how I want my mate presenting herself. Once we are mated, you'll change it back to a natural color."

What was it with these men and their obsession with my hair? "I'm not changing it, and we aren't mated, Neil."

"Not yet," he said, smirking. I let out a deep breath, trying to just let it go.

Finally, after what felt like an hour but was actually only ten minutes, we arrived. I gathered myself and turned to open the door.

"Thanks for the ride, Neil. I was lucky that you happened to be nearby."

"You could thank me by letting me take you to dinner," he suggested. I gave a half-hearted laugh before I realized that he was being serious.

"You probably didn't get my text, Neil, but I need a few days to unwind first. Let's make a date for next week, okay?"

I was almost out of the car when he reached for my arm. I stilled, but my wolf was ready to pounce. Something in his touch felt vaguely threatening.

"Jeremy suggested that we take things slow, seeing as how you just recently decided to forgo your *true mate*," Neil spat. He said the words 'true mate' like Gabe was some kind of social pariah. "I told him that wouldn't be necessary because we are alike, you and me. I've felt that from the first moment we met, Ella. We like things to be in order, a hierarchy. It's what separates wolves from other shifters, you know?"

Hoping that was the end, I nodded, but he wasn't finished. "This will work out; you'll see. And I'll forgive you for turning down dinner this time, but just know that once you are mine, saying no to anything won't be an option anymore."

Chapter 10

Well, that was weird.

I closed the door behind me, immediately locking it for good measure.

I didn't think Neil would resort to breaking and entering, but his parting words put me on edge. He was someone to trust, though. Maybe I was overreacting, but something inside told me I probably wasn't.

We need our mate. You should beg him to take us back. My wolf swung her tail low, miffed at the strange beta telling us what to do, but not threatened enough to try and force a shift. She recognized his leadership in the pack, his place as our beta, but that didn't mean she enjoyed him asserting himself above us in a personal sense. I had to agree with her on that.

Still, it didn't mean I was going to agree about contacting Gabe. Her wolf brain didn't understand things like social awkwardness or humiliation. In her mind, Gabe was ours, and staking our claim on him against Samantha was the most natural thing in the world, regardless of what Gabe or I wanted. I wondered if that would change at all after he decided to break our bond. Would it change for her instantly, like flipping a light switch? Or would she need to see him in person to know it was over? Would I even know when it happened without ever seeing him again?

For some reason, the thought of never seeing Gabe's smile again made me inexplicably sad. Maybe after he was mated to Samantha, we would be able to be friends or something like that. When I returned to Tumblewild to visit Mariam, I would imagine he would be around, too.

If I ever visit Mariam. *If* a mate like Neil would even allow me to do that. I sighed and put on the kettle for some tea.

I was being ridiculous. This was what I had wanted, basically; some strict, authoritarian mate who wasn't a pushover to come and take charge. Neil certainly wasn't a pushover, but he wasn't really what I had imagined, either. His brand of control was cold like I was just another subordinate who should follow his orders because he was a hotshot beta. It's not like he acted bossy toward me because he had any feelings for me or because we were mates or anything like that. I couldn't even imagine kissing him, much less consummating the relationship with sex and a mating bite.

I had to admit, begrudging, that with Gabe, I was ready to jump his bones the second he kissed me. Despite every attempt to talk myself out of wanting him, I couldn't help myself. Even the parts of him that had seemed undesirable to me at first now made me want to throw myself at him even more.

The hot tea helped calm my nerves like always, but I didn't even crack open the book sitting on the side table. I remember being miffed at the airport because I had forgotten it, and now finishing it felt inconsequential. I curled up under a throw blanket that belonged to my mother, breathing in deeply as I fell asleep. It used to smell like her at one time, but now it just smelled like laundry detergent.

The dreams I had been having were weird, and this one was no different. I couldn't tell where I was except that it was indoors. It felt dark outside, and other people were around me. Other werewolves, I should say. Someone was talking, but their words were muffled and impossible to understand.

A second voice joined in, and the two of them started arguing. One of the voices was deep, and the other spoke with a higher pitch. It was a male and female, but that was about all I could figure out.

I strained to hear more. Whenever I started to make out a few words, it was like someone increased the volume on a noise machine to drown them out again. I tossed and turned for hours, waking only when I fell off the couch and landed with a thud on the ground.

Groaning, I rubbed my forehead and sat up. My heart was pounding in my chest, and my eyes were wide with fear. Everything I heard felt so real, and I couldn't shake the feeling that it was more than a dream.

I glanced at my phone and shock set it when I realized I had slept through the rest of the afternoon, and it was almost eight in the evening. And yet, somehow, I felt more exhausted than when I had first arrived home.

As I stood up and stretched, I heard a knock on the door, likely the same sound that had caused me to wake up in the first place.

I tiptoed to the door, listening carefully for any sounds outside. I peeked through the peephole and saw a tall, dark figure fill the porch.

My heart raced as I recognized the silhouette. It was Gabe. He stood there, his hands shoved into the pockets of his leather jacket, looking down at his feet. I hesitated for a moment, unsure of what to do. Should I open the door? Or should I stay inside and pretend not to be home?

But before I could make a decision, Gabe spoke up. "Ella, I know you're in there. Can we talk? Please?"

His voice was calm, but there was a hint of desperation in it that made my heart ache. I took a deep breath and unlocked the door, pulling it open slowly. I was instantly hit with the comforting cinnamon scent that I had come to associate with him.

"What do you want?" I asked, keeping my voice steady.

He looked up at me, his eyes intense. "I need to talk to you."

I hesitated for a moment before stepping aside, allowing him to enter. He walked past me, his eyes taking in the family pictures on the wall. His lips twitched, forming a small smile at one of Mariam and me at the beach before our mom got sick. I closed the door behind him, leaning against it as I watched him enter the living room.

"What's going on, Gabe?" I asked, keeping my distance. "What are you even doing in Dark Claw?"

He ran a hand through his hair, looking up at me with a mix of pain and regret. "I made a mistake, Ella. A huge mistake. Or more like several mistakes, really, and I need to fix them."

My heart skipped a beat as I stared at him, not sure what

he was talking about. "What mistakes?"

He took a deep breath, his eyes never leaving mine. "Letting you leave., for one. I told myself I would wait for you to decide to return on your own, but that's not what you need from me. And besides that, I screwed up big time by trusting Samantha and making you think that you couldn't trust me to be faithful to you. All those things add up to be the biggest mistakes of my life, and I can't let you go without knowing that this is really, truly what you want."

I blinked, unsure of what to say. This wasn't what I expected at all.

"There really isn't anything to apologize for, Gabe. You were with Samantha long before we met, and it would be wrong for me to try and take you from her."

Gabe's eyes flashed. "You don't have anything to worry about with Samantha," he grumbled. "I spoke with her, and she admitted to misleading you about our friendship. She's had a crush on me for a while, but I never thought she would do anything like that. Sometimes I just see the best in people and ignore everything else, I suppose."

I blinked, trying to process what he was saying. Samantha had lied to me? Gabe had been faithful to me all along? It was too much to take in all at once.

"Gabe, I don't know what to say," I admitted. "I thought you were with her. I thought you didn't want me. But even if you might be interested...well, I don't know."

He reached out, taking my hand in his. "I never stopped wanting you, Ella. I just thought this was what you wanted. I was trying to respect your wishes, even if it meant letting you go. But after feeling the loss of you leaving… it was worse than I thought it would be. I couldn't stay away."

His admission seemed to steal the last of his self-control, and the next thing I knew, he was pushing me up against the wall, his lips pressed firmly on mine. His hands roamed over my body, kneading the curves of my hips, waist, and breasts. I groaned and opened my mouth to deepen the kiss.

I sucked in a breath as I felt his canines elongate. The mixture of pleasure and pain they created against my lips caused a tugging sensation to grow in my tummy and travel to my core. I rubbed myself against him, trying to satisfy the growing pressure. He nipped along my jaw until his fangs found the sensitive spot on my neck, right above my clavicle.

My knees buckled when he ran a sharpened tooth there, sending tremors through me and causing more liquid heat to pool between my legs. My wolf was pushing to the front, eager to accept his bite.

I was close to begging him for a mating bite when another knock on the door shook me out of the stupor. Gabe jumped and blinked down at me, fighting to take control back from his wolf.

The knocking grew louder, angrier. It was clear that whoever was on my front porch wasn't going away. I pushed against Gabe's chest, creating space for me to go and answer it. He groaned before reluctantly letting me move away from him.

"Are you expecting someone?" he asked, following me to the front door. It was already getting dark outside, so the question might be strictly about safety, but there was a slight sharpness in his voice.

I scoffed at the idea that Gabe could be jealous. It's not like I had a male Samantha hanging around hoping to become my mate.

I spoke too soon. My eyes widened when I checked to see who was knocking. Standing on the front porch, looking impatient and slightly perturbed, was Neil. I backed away from the door and shot Gabe a panicked glance.

"Listen, I'm sorry, but I need you to get out of here," I hissed. Neil growled on the other side of the door, likely able to hear exactly what I was saying. Not for the first time, I silently cursed heightened werewolf hearing abilities.

Gabe quirked an eyebrow and shook his head. It was hard to tell if he was pissed off or amused. "I'm not leaving you here with another male, so you might as well just open the door, mate."

I rolled my eyes and opened the door, bracing myself for Neil to try and push his way into the room, but it didn't happen. His face was contorted with rage when his eyes flitted briefly to Gabe, but then the expression completely disappeared when his gaze landed on me. I didn't get his anger, but I also didn't receive any affection. He looked utterly emotionless.

"Ella," he said in a firm voice no louder than a whisper. "I wanted to update you about your car and take you to dinner. Go and get ready. I'll wait here for you to freshen up."

His nostrils flared and looking closely, I could see a tell. His jaw ticked, betraying how upset he was. My cheeks flamed when I realized what he was saying. He could smell Gabe's scent on me, and now he wanted me to go and wash it off. Either that or it was my arousal that upset him. In all likelihood, he could probably scent both mixed together.

I hesitated, unsure of what to do or say. I felt guilty being caught with Gabe in the house, which was ridiculous. Neil and I hadn't even been on a single date yet. But having a male alone in the house felt too risqué for me anyway.

Neil reached up to touch the flush on my cheeks again, but this time I didn't push him away. "Be a good girl and do as I asked."

My heart melted at the words. They were the same ones Dad used to use with Mom when he was being affectionate. "Give me a few minutes. I'll come out, and then we can talk about the car. Thanks for taking care of that, Neil."

I tried to close the door again, but he caught it with his hand. Neil's eyes were squarely on Gabe now.

"Give me a minute with your... friend. I'm sure we can find something to talk about while you get ready."

Gabe stood his ground, not backing away from Neil's intimidating presence. In fact, he seemed to be challenging him back, chest puffed out, and eyes narrowed in indignation. Gabe gave me a tight smile and nodded that he was fine waiting with Neil. "We've met before, actually," he said.

"Fine," I said, opening the door wider. "I'll just be a minute."

I turned and went to my bedroom, feeling the tension between them like a heavy fog. My adrenaline was pumping, making me feel strangely alive. I could still hear their muffled voices as I went up the stairs, but I couldn't make out what they were saying.

When I got to my room, I shut the door behind me, then leaned against it with a sigh of relief. The air felt different here in my haven, lighter and calmer than what was going on downstairs.

Stripping off my clothes, I stepped inside the stall and let the warm water cascade down my body. The scent of lavender and rosemary from the body wash filled the steamy air, but I didn't allow myself to savor the feeling. I scrubbed Gabe's scent from my skin and hair. Especially my hair, where he had fisted the curls with his hand. The memory of his body pushed up against mine was enough to make me weak again, but I refused to get lost in the sensation. I quickly finished getting washed and dressed before returning downstairs, nervous about what I would find.

My pulse quickened as I came to the bottom of the stairs. Neil was standing in the living room with his hands in his pockets, and Gabe was sitting on the couch, flipping through the book I had left on the coffee table. I suppose I should be thankful that no one was fighting. Maybe I had misread the tension that I had felt.

"Ready?" Neil asked me. Once again, his words felt less like a question and more like a statement. I almost rolled my eyes, but something stopped me from doing so. I glanced at Gabe.

"Sorry, but I probably need to check on my car. It broke down, and Neil helped me get it looked at."

"It's fine, Ella. I'll be here when you get back. We'll talk more then." Gabe leaned into the couch, making himself comfortable.

If Neil heard him, it didn't show. Instead, the beta reached for my hand and led us to the front door.

I paused and turned back to Gabe. "Okay, I'll be back soon. If you're hungry or anything, there's —"

Neil let out a low growl deep in the back of his throat. The sound snapped Gabe to attention, breaking the air of indifference he had put on.

I quickly patted Neil on the shoulders, trying to laugh off the possessive noises coming from him like it was all a big joke. "Okay, sounds good. See you later, Gabe."

Neil and I got into his truck, but before we even made it out of the driveway, he rounded on me. "What the hell was that?" he spat, anger filling his voice.

I narrowed my eyes at him in response. "Neil, we aren't together. We haven't even gone on a date yet. I don't know what you're freaking out about."

"A date?" he repeated quietly. His eyes searched my face. "Ella, I'm interested in you because I know you value the traditional roles of our kind. Werewolves don't date. It would go against everything in our DNA. I'll agree to a short courting period if you think that's necessary, but honestly, that shouldn't be a requirement, either. Male werewolves claim their mates, and when they aren't strong enough to do that, females end up with losers like the one sitting on your couch."

My wolf's anger rose to the surface at his disrespect toward our mate. I tried to suppress her, but it was no use.

"Our male is more than sufficient. He's our perfect match," she snapped through me.

"If you really believed that you wouldn't be leaving with me," Neil answered her. "There's a reason you don't want to be with him, even with the true mate draw. Call me crazy, Ella, but I think you know what you need, and that isn't him."

Neil backed the truck out of the driveway and drove toward town. Silence filled the cab, creating an even bigger distance between us. I couldn't argue with what he said but agreeing with him felt like a huge betrayal to Gabe, especially after the explosive makeup session.

The memory of his teeth on my skin and his hardness between my legs caused my heart to beat faster. I squirmed in my seat, awkward over being turned on.

Suddenly, Neil pulled over to the shoulder, and before I could process what was happening, he was on top of me. His hands skimmed over my seatbelt, clicking it free and pulling me close.

"Ella, I can feel the way you want this. I know you can feel it too." His lips were tantalizingly close to mine, and a wave of warmth flooded my body. "Let me show you what being truly claimed feels like."

I instinctually melted into his embrace, overwhelmed by the sensations coursing through my veins. I wanted to give in and feel the possessive heat of his kiss, but my wolf sprung forward.

"Enough. You are not our mate, beta," she said through my lips. Her glare froze his hands, calling to the animal inside him.

I watched his eyes shift and become animal, too.

"My human wants to claim yours, but I can scent the other male on you," the wolf ground out. "You are still tied to him, female."

The words were an apology with rough edges, the only kind that would be expected from a beta like Neil. Apparently, his wolf was used to getting his way, too, but at least he was respecting the fundamental boundaries of our kind.

Basically, don't mess with another wolf's mate.

An understanding passed between our wolves before they both backed off. At least I wouldn't have to worry about Neil claiming me then and there; his wolf didn't want to touch me as long as the connection between Gabe and I remained intact.

I waited for the last of the animal's glow to leave Neil's eyes before I pushed him off of me, more conscious than ever of the proximity of our bodies. The absence of his weight left me a little empty. Despite my conflicted feelings, it had felt good to hold the large male against my body. *Maybe this was what Mariam had meant when she talked about the perks of taking more than one lover.*

I shook my head to rid myself of the scandalous thought.

"Take me home, Neil," I said. "I can pick up my car from Patrick on my own in the morning."

Chapter 11

I scowled at Neil. As the pack's beta, wasn't he supposed to be as least somewhat intelligent? "What do you mean, no?"

"You heard me," he said. "No. I'm not taking you back. We're going to pick up your car. I had Patrick deliver it to my house because he was closing up the garage, and I didn't want you to be without it over the weekend."

Oh. Right. I had forgotten it was Friday, but it hadn't occurred to me that the auto shop would be closed for the weekend anyway.

I sighed, relenting a little at his thoughtfulness. He threw me a conspirator's grin, clearly enjoying my conceding to his plan. All traces of irritation over being rejected seemed to disappear, almost like it never happened.

"Fine. We can go get my car, but that's it. I appreciate you helping me as a member of the pack, but clearly, this thing between us isn't going to work out. I'm sorry I wasted your time."

Neil snorted. "Is that what you think? Ella, nothing has changed for me. Sure, my wolf is hesitant because you smell like that asshole on your couch, but that's a problem I can handle. He's an omega and a pretty laidback one at that. I bet if you told him you want to break your mating bond, he would roll over and do it."

I looked away. Gabe would break our bond if I asked him to. He had said as much already. Did I really want to be mated to someone who would give me up so easily? Neil smiled and took my hand, enveloping it in his larger one. "I've been waiting for someone like you, a female who wants the discipline and structure that someone like me can offer."

Something in me wanted to protest, but a bigger part couldn't deny how my heart somersaulted when Neil took control. Something about his easy possessiveness was appealing, as much as it felt weird to admit. I chewed on my lip and frowned.

His eyes darkened as they landed on my mouth, but he didn't try to cross the center consul again. I doubted his wolf would let him, anyway.

"You'll see, Ella. You'll be my good girl, and I'll be the man you need to keep you in line."

The words were both a promise and a threat, and I shivered at the intensity of his voice. Why did it feel like he could look inside my head and know exactly what I wanted to hear?

"Come on," he said, snapping me out of my trance. "Let's go get your car."

I nodded, still slightly in shock from the impact of his words. Neil must have sensed my apprehension because he squeezed my hand reassuringly before shifting into gear and guiding us back onto the road. The drive to Neil's house was surprisingly short, given how much tension filled the air between us.

I don't know exactly what I was expecting, but for some reason, I hadn't considered that he would be living with Jeremy in the alpha house. Unlike Tumblewild, the alpha house in Dark Claw wasn't much bigger than a typical home. From the outside, I would've guessed it was about 3,000 square feet, with maybe five bedrooms. It certainly wasn't large enough for the last leadership team to live together, which led to the pack administration building another house down the street for the former beta couple. But then again, the former alpha and beta both had families. Maybe this was just a temporary situation until Jeremy and Neil found mates and had kids of their own.

Neil seemed to be dead set on finding a mate, at least.

I could feel Neil's gaze, almost like he was reading my thoughts.

"Thanks for the ride and for getting my car," I said. "Do you have my keys?"

"I do. Just know that after we're mated, that hunk of junk is being replaced with something new and safe." He handed me the keys, completely unaware of how upset I was becoming.

"Well, thanks again," I choked out. I hurried to exit the truck and beelined to my car, grateful to be back inside the familiar space again. To anyone else, it probably *was* just a hunk of junk, but the car also belonged to my mother, and I wasn't getting rid of it. No matter who I ended up mated to. I brushed away the tears forming in my eyes, angry with myself over how defensive I was over a silly car.

Neil tapped gently on the window, but I didn't bother rolling it down. I could hear him fine through the glass. "I'm sorry if I hurt your feelings, Ella. I just want you to be safe. I'll have a room ready for your friend at the Feldman Hotel. Send him over there when you get home."

I opened my mouth to protest, but Neil's growl stopped the words from forming. "My future mate isn't spending the night with another male. Either you're staying here, or he's leaving. Don't make me go and get you. I'll be waiting for confirmation that he's checked in from the front desk. If I don't hear from them soon, you should pack a bag for yourself because I'll be on my way over. Otherwise, I'll pick you up after work so we can have a proper meal together."

For the first time I could remember, I struggled not to give someone my middle finger. Instead, I nodded curtly and turned over the car. Thankfully, it came to life without issue.

"I mean it, Ella."

I pulled away from the alpha house without answering. Despite the horrible feeling that I was betraying Gabe, every part of my body hummed with the guilty pleasure of receiving the possessive instructions. Maybe Neil was right. Maybe I was meant for someone like him.

———————

I'm not sure what I expected to find when I got home, but Gabe pretty much hadn't moved from the couch. He was almost halfway through the book and barely glanced my way when I walked in. The only sign that anything was amiss was the stark whites of his knuckles that stood out from gripping the pages too hard.

Gabe didn't say anything until I was standing in front of him, and then he finally looked up with an unreadable expression. "You took a while. What happened?"

I took a deep breath and told him the whole story, including my wolf speaking with Neil's and the confusion I felt over what to do. Gabe listened without interruption, his face changing from confusion to disbelief and then to sadness as I spoke. When I finished recounting the events, Gabe stood up from the couch and began pacing around the room.

"So, you're just going to let him tell you what to do?" he whispered. "You're just going to sit there and take orders from him? Ella, I'm trying to be understanding, I want to be patient with you, but you have to know... my wolf is telling me in no uncertain terms to go and rip his throat out."

My eyes widened at the threat. This was not the Gabe that I knew. I doubt it was the person Mariam had come to talk about as a brother, either. And despite the violence in his words, his voice hadn't raised a single octave.

"Do you have feelings for him, Ella? He's practically a caveman, you know. Before Randy came along, he practically forced himself on Justine at one point."

I knit my brows together. "That's a pretty serious accusation. Are you sure?"

Gabe let out a slow breath. "I mean, I wasn't there to see it, but Justine messed him up over it. They had lunch together, and I guess he wanted her to be his mate."

I scoffed. Justine was known for her short temper, and I could easily imagine her starting a fight if Neil became a little too friendly. That wasn't as concerning as the idea of the beta barging in and taking me to the alpha house, so it seemed like there was only one solution.

"Neil got you a hotel room at the Feldman. I think you should stay there tonight," I said. "We'll talk tomorrow when I get off of work."

It looked like Gabe was going to argue about leaving, but then he took a deep breath and nodded. As I watched him leave, a strange feeling bubbled up in my chest. I couldn't help but feel some kind of connection to Neil. Was it just the animalistic nature of our wolves coming out, an attraction just because his creature was dominant and mine was more submissive? Or was it something deeper?

Was I falling for him?

I shook my head and tried to push the thought away. It couldn't be possible. Before yesterday, we had only spoken a handful of times, tops. But still, the feeling lingered and seemed to grow with each passing moment.

It was unsettling and confusing but also strangely exciting at the same time. I had never felt this way about anyone before, and part of me wanted to explore these feelings further. Maybe it was because no one had ever felt this way about me. Least of all, Gabe, as he left without another word. If their places were switched and Neil was my true mate, Gabe would have given me up without so much as a second thought. Maybe what Neil was showing me was real love. Real passion.

Surely there must be something more between us than simple, instinctual attraction?

But how could I know unless I took a chance?

The drive to the hotel had felt surreal, almost like Gabe

was watching it happen from the outside. He hadn't expected Ella to jump into his arms and beg for him to bite her— okay, maybe he was hoping for something like that, but it was alright if she wanted to take things slow. Gabe could be understanding, reassuring... he could be whatever she needed him to be.

Instead, some random asshole was already moving in on her. *Neil*. His name was irritating enough, which was totally unfair, but at this point, Gabe didn't even care anymore. Neil was after his true mate. Niceties would have to wait until he and Ella could sort things out.

We should go back and claim our female, his wolf grumbled. *She would want us to do so. She was willing before the imposter male arrived.*

Their shared memory flashed before his eyes. Ella had been more than ready when they were kissing in her house. She had been so compliant and wet; the scent of her arousal had been pure heaven. Just the thought of it made Gabe's dick rock hard again.

Great. Now he'd have to check into the Feldman sporting a raging boner.

Gabe stepped out of the car, bag in hand. When he packed it, he thought he would be staying with Ella. Hopefully, this would just be for one night, and then they could pick up where they'd left off. He started walking up the stairs but froze halfway up. Leaning against one of the entrance pillars, arms folded, was Neil.

"It's good you got here when you did, friend. I would have hated to ask our alpha to escort you off pack land."

Gabe bit back a retort. He couldn't be sure if the threat was legitimate, but he wasn't going to risk being separated from Ella just to prove a point. Judging from Neil's smirk, the beta had anticipated that already.

Gabe was going to walk by without taking the bait, but as he moved to pass, Neil unfolded his arms and blocked his path to the registration desk.

"I got you a room for the evening, but let's have dinner in the restaurant first. My treat."

"Thanks, but I think I'm good," Gabe said, meeting Neil's eyes and refusing to be the first to look away. As an omega, it wasn't easy holding the oppressive stare of a beta, and Neil seemed a little impressed when he didn't back down.

"It wasn't a suggestion, Gabriel," Neil said, his voice low so no one else could hear. "Let's go to dinner, and then I'll let you get some rest."

Gabe's irritation rose but showing his emotions wouldn't do any good. When the beta of a pack wanted to have a meal with you, you had the meal. He nodded curtly and handed his bag to the bellhop, who materialized out of thin air when Neil gestured for someone to help.

He followed Neil to the left-hand side of the hotel, through the high arches, and into the dining area. In the back, there was a private room, which was already set for two. Gabe pulled up a chair at the place setting Neil indicated, then cut to the chase.

"So, what do you need to say to me? If you want me to give up my bond with Ella, you're wasting your time."

Neil sighed and snapped his napkin open, resting it on his knee. Gabe remained still, keeping his eyes on the other shifter rather than the spread of food.

"Gabe, you seem like a nice guy. We have a few omegas

in our pack that remind me of you," Neil said, picking up his knife and fork to slice into his steak. "They're reliable, fair, and very trustworthy. I'm sure if I were to ask around about you, everyone would probably say the same things, right?"

Gabe kept his face neutral and waited for Neil to continue. He seemed like someone who enjoyed hearing himself speak.

As it turns out, he didn't expect an answer, anyway. Neil just nodded to himself and continued talking. "What I'm saying, Gabe, is that in a pack, omegas are very valuable members, but there's a reason they usually mate with other omegas. Females like Ella require something different. They need a firmer hand. They thrive on it. It's not your fault you can't give her what she needs. Hell, you don't even understand what she needs."

A small voice in his head agreed with Neil, and that made him see red. He had to be enough for her. There was no other option.

"You think you know her, but I can give her the love and protection she deserves. That's why we're true mates," Gabe argued, breaking his silence. "Besides, if you think she's so special, why did you wait until now to do anything about it? She's lived here her whole life."

Neil grimaced. "That was a mistake on my part. I'd been so busy looking for a mate outside our pack that it never occurred to me that I could find a worthy one here. Besides, I'm sure you've heard stories about how promiscuous Mariam was. I assumed her sister would have participated in similar... activities."

"You want her now because you know she's a virgin?"

Gabe spat. The thought made his hackles rise. The thought of this idiot trying to get with his mate just to sleep with her had him reeling.

"Interesting. Is that important to you, Gabe? That she be a virgin?" Neil asked. He tilted his head thoughtfully and took a bite of mashed potatoes. "For me, that's just a matter of probability. I don't know what it's like where you're from, but most shifters in Dark Claw are chaste before mating. The females are, anyway. What makes Ella special is something that Jeremy pointed out after spending time with her recently. Unlike many females in our time, she doesn't just accept a mate's domination; she's looking forward to it. I'm sure I don't have to explain why that's appealing." He paused, looking the omega over thoughtfully. "Or maybe I do."

"I think I've heard enough," Gabe snapped. "I'm not going to explain to you how strong a true mating bond is or why you should be respecting it. You can talk all you want about dominance and submission, but if you don't respect those basic tenants of our kind, there's really no helping you. After Justine rejected you, I'm sure your pride is bruised, but I don't really care how you feel. You might want Ella, but I'd kill for her."

Neil folded his napkin, sighing. "I really do wish you the best, Gabe. I meant what I said about you being a good omega. But I don't think you truly understand how this will play out, and for that, I'm sorry. I thought I was clear when we spoke back at Ella's house."

He clapped Gabe on the shoulder and opened the door to let himself out.

"By the way," Neil said, pausing as he stepped onto the

restaurant floor. "I have a few people here at the hotel tonight, so don't even think about going back to Ella's house. Her virginity isn't the only thing on my mind, but I'll spill your blood if she smells like you ever again."

Gabe sat in silence after Neil left, debating whether it was worth it to go back to Ella's house and cause her a bunch of problems. Outside, the streetlights were on, and she had mentioned going to work in the morning. Working at a bakery probably meant early hours. Staying at the hotel for the night could be the best move, even if everything in him wanted to storm back to her.

He ran his hands through his hair again before taking his phone out of his pocket and dialing Mariam. Gabe wasn't sure if she'd have any words of wisdom on handling her former beta or proving himself to her sister, but he was getting desperate for some help.

Chapter 12

For the second time that day, I found myself lost in thought in the shower. The warm water wasn't as wonderful as the first time, or maybe my brain was too jumbled to enjoy it. Hopefully, I will get some rest tonight. I was willing to trade pretty much anything to avoid the weird dreams that plagued my mind the past few nights.

I stepped out of the shower and wrapped myself in the towel I had hung on the back of the door. I used a second one to wipe some fog from the mirror. I stood there, staring at my reflection. I wondered why both shifters were suddenly so interested in me when no one had even looked my way up until now. I was at least average looking, sure, but so were most other female werewolves.

My wolf didn't care about how my human form looked one bit. *We shouldn't have let our mate leave*, she huffed. She was more than ready to put the whole Samantha issue behind us and ask for Gabe's mating bite. But the more I thought about it, the less sure I was about it.

The little things were nagging at me. Like Gabe being resigned to stay at the hotel when Trace or Neil or any other shifter male wouldn't have agreed to those terms for one minute. Was that proof that maybe they weren't true mates after all? The only thing I was going off of was the scent of cinnamon and Gabe's word that we were meant to be together. What if he was wrong?

I sighed, knowing that there were no answers to all of this. I quickly brushed my teeth and gargled with mouthwash, happy to leave my distorted reflection behind. I padded barefoot back into my bedroom and traded the towel for a fluffy robe. My book was still downstairs, but I didn't care. All I wanted was some sleep.

I was asleep the second my head hit the pillow. I slept soundly for a few minutes, but then the same male voice was back. He was talking to someone, a different female than last time, but this conversation was much clearer. It was Gabe, and he was having a video chat with Mariam. I could see her. I could see the entire hotel room he was sitting in. It was as though I was looking through Gabe's eyes.

I could also feel what he was feeling; his anxiety was enough to put my stomach into knots.

Poor Gabe. My wolf whined in agreement.

I wanted to comfort him. I needed to help him somehow, but I also didn't want to interrupt his conversation with my sister, although it might be too late for that. He let her finish what she was saying, something about Neil and that he needed to be careful, but then he abruptly cut her off.

"Sorry, Mariam. I need to go, but I'll call as soon as I have any news."

"You better," she teased. "Tell Ella hi for me. She's being a *great* sister and still not returning any of my calls or texts. I hope to see you both back in Tumblewild soon. It's lonely here without you!"

Gabe tapped to end the call. *Is that you, Ella?*

His thoughts appeared in my mind as if they were my own. *What's going on, Gabe? This is the weirdest dream I've ever had.*

That was an understatement. Sharing a mind, one consciousness, with Gabe was not what I had planned when I went to bed.

It's not a dream, he answered. *But don't worry. It's a good thing, actually. True mates can tap into each other's thoughts after they claim each other.*

I frowned. Was I missing something here? We hadn't completed the bite or consummated anything. Why was this happening now?

Gabe chuckled. Of course, he had heard my line of questioning, too.

Something similar happened to Mariam and Trace when their mating was delayed. I read something about it a while back when she was going through it and freaking out. It would only happen when one of them was asleep. The other could see into their world, and as soon as their union was consummated, I guess their connection changed to what other true mates experienced.

I didn't respond right away, trying to figure out what this would mean for us. Most importantly, it was proof that we were true mates after all, although that's assuming Gabe wasn't making that part up...

You can ask Mariam. I'm sure she would confirm that this happened to her, as well.

I winced. His feelings were hurt that I was doubting him again, but he was the one who told me Samantha was only a friend.

Which is 100% true, by the way, he interjected.

I sighed. Having another person in my head was complicating things. *I'm going to need you to stop reading my mind so I can organize my thoughts, Gabe.*

There is a way to sever the connection, he said reluctantly. *But do you really want to do that? I'm enjoying this with you, Ella. We haven't had a lot of time to just talk to each other.*

I know. I'm sorry. I'm just so tired, and last night I couldn't sleep because I heard you talking with another person, and the arguing kept me awake.

What other person? he asked, curious. *When did you hear me? Could you tell what I was saying?*

No, I replied. *It wasn't clear enough to hear anything other than to know it was a female's voice and that you were arguing.*

Oh, I think I know. He paused for a moment but then showed me the memory of him talking on the phone with Samantha. They were arguing about what she had said to me.

I called her on my way to your house after I had landed. Mariam thought she might have said something misleading to you when you were at the diner, and it turns out she was right.

I wasn't sure what to say. The memory was proof that some kind of argument had happened between the two of them, but my brain was fuzzy from lack of sleep.

I really need to get some rest for work tomorrow. Can we block this connection for now?

Yes. He sighed. *Goodnight, Ella. I wish I was there with you.*

Goodnight, Gabe. And thank you.

The silence that filled my mind was more than welcome, and I was finally able to drift off into a heavy sleep.

My alarm going off made me question how much I liked my job. I groaned, fumbling with my phone in the dark. Normally, I woke up a few minutes before it started beeping, but I had tried to squeeze in every second of sleep I could before forcing myself to get ready for work.

Now, at 3 am, I donned my typical jeans and t-shirt along with my apron and non-slip clogs. I set my hair in a bun, brushed my teeth, and even applied a little concealer and mascara.

My phone dinged with a text from Gabe.

Hope you slept well and that you have a good day at work. Missing you.

His thoughtfulness brought a smile to my lips.

I grabbed my keys and drove to the bakery, thankful for the quiet roads. I arrived a few minutes early, but Heather was already working and had completed several items on the morning routine. The smell of fresh donuts wafted through the air and made my stomach growl. She handed me a pastry with a cup of coffee from the pot that was perpetually brewing.

The price of those items was an update on my love life, apparently.

"Gabe's in town. He's staying at the Feldman," I said between bites. "I guess I'm having lunch with Neil, but I'll probably need to break things off with him."

"Really? Why the sudden change of mind?" Heather's eyes sparkled. She was enjoying the drama of the situation a little too much, but she didn't mean any harm. Like me, she was impatiently waiting for a true mate and was using the situation to live vicariously through me.

"I was able to confirm that Gabe's my true mate last

night and that what Samantha told me about them dating was a lie, so I guess we should try to work things out. We were put together for a reason, after all." I shrugged like it didn't matter, but the truth was this felt like a huge decision. If things didn't work out with Gabe, I might end up just being alone and never having a mate or kids. Family was important to shifters, and I could almost feel the time on my biological clock ticking away.

Plus, Neil probably wasn't going to take rejection well, and I wasn't looking forward to that conversation one bit. Heather seemed to understand my unsaid concerns and gave me a small hug before getting back to work.

The routine of opening the bakery helped with my anxiety. Soon we were in a rhythm, working side-by-side, humming and restocking ingredients. When that was done, we worked in tandem -- me prepping more pastries while she handled the breads -- until we were ready to open just before sunrise.

As customers began streaming in, we traded off baking what we had prepped and helping customers. By noon I was still humming, particularly from the coffee and sugar, but mostly because I was dreading going to lunch.

I clocked out and changed out of my apron as a text came through.

Neil: I was held up with some pack business. I'm on my way to the bakery now.

Me: Okay, just got off. I'll meet you outside.

I sighed aloud as I hit send and slipped my phone into my purse. Heather eyed me carefully, taking off her own apron and packing up to leave.

"Do you want me to wait with you? Or go with you,

even? I've heard that Neil can be a little on the... difficult side, you know? When he's disappointed or upset."

"I'm sure it will be fine. We've only talked about going out for the past few days. It's not like this news is going to devastate him or anything. Besides, I'm going to take my own car, so if things go wrong, at least I can make a quick getaway."

I intended it to be a joke, but Heather didn't smile, instead nodding stiffly.

"I'll keep my phone on me in case you need some backup," she said.

Neil was already waiting outside, arms crossed with a slight scowl on his face.

"Sorry about being a little late," he said, straightening up when he saw me. He opened the passenger door of his truck and gestured for me to get inside.

"I think it would be better for us to drive separately, Neil. That way, after lunch, you don't have to take me back here," I said. It wasn't a lie, but I knew I wasn't being smooth about it, either. Neil must have thought so, too, because he cocked a brow at me.

"Everything alright?" he asked.

"Yes, everything's fine. Where do you want to have lunch?"

"Well, first, I want you to get in, and then we can talk about lunch."

I chewed on my lip, unsure of what to do.

"Hey, Ella. I just remembered that Marissa needed you to cover her shift this afternoon. Do you think you can stick around for a little bit?"

Heather appeared on my right, as if materializing from

thin air. Neil turned his attention to her, his eyes frosty.

"Unfortunately, we have plans," he said.

I smiled at Heather and gave her hand a quick squeeze. "Sorry, I can't today, but I'll text you after I have lunch with Neil and see if you still need me to come in."

Heather sighed but nodded and told us to have a good time.

I watched her walking away, weighing my options. The ride home afterward might be awkward, but if I refused to ride with Neil, he would be in an even worse mood.

"Fine," I said. "Let's go." My wolf whined and paced, unhappy to be alone with the other male.

Ignoring her, I buckled my seatbelt and asked again. "So. Where are we going for lunch?"

"I wanted to take you back to my place. Alpha house," Neil said, looking behind us as he pulled out of the parking spot. "Jeremy is out of town, and I want you to see the inside. We won't have to live there after our mating ceremony, but in some ways, it is easier for me to be onsite in case Jeremy needs me for something."

I let out a slow breath. I guess having this conversation couldn't wait. "Listen, we need to talk about all this, Neil. I don't think...I mean, I think I need to see where things go with Gabe before I think about pursuing something with anyone else. I thought for sure we weren't going to be a good fit for each other, but since he's been here, things have changed." I paused. "Plus, I don't think we would be right for each other anyway. I'm really sorry I wasted your time."

At first, I thought that maybe Neil didn't hear me, but when he parked in front of Alpha house, it was clear that he heard every word.

"Ella, I've said this before, and I guess I need to say it again. The kind of thing that we can have is pretty special. I've searched all over for a female who desires a more traditional relationship, but I never expected to find you here, inside Dark Claw, all along. We can break the bond you have already and live a happy life here. You can continue working at the bakery, and you'll have a mate who cares about you. And better yet, who understands you and what you need. Gabriel, as nice as he is, can't give you that."

I started to protest, but he cut me off. "Fine. I get it. You love Gabe or whatever. Just come inside and have the lunch I prepared for us."

I gave him a weary look but nodded. If he had gone to all the trouble to actually cook something, the least I could do was eat it. My wolf whined, torn between following the orders of the beta and just wanting to go see Gabe.

I followed Neil up the walk and inside. I looked around as he hung up my coat, surprised to find a well-appointed foyer and sitting room. The place looked really nice for housing two single males.

"Were you expecting pizza boxes and beer cans?" Neil teased.

I laughed and shrugged. "I wasn't expecting Scandinavian rugs and candles, I guess."

"The house was decorated by Jeremy's mom, and we haven't really changed anything since he took over as alpha," Neil answered, chuckling. "She had good taste. What can I say?"

He led me to the kitchen and started unpacking some

tubs from the fridge.

"I prepared a few things ahead of time last night, but the rest shouldn't take too long," he said. "Sit and keep me company while I cook."

I sat on a barstool, watching Neil pull out a large pot and start boiling water for pasta. He was quick and efficient, chopping vegetables and grating cheese with practiced ease. It was kind of impressive, actually. I'd never met a man who was so skilled in the kitchen.

I cleared my throat, feeling awkward. "So... how's pack business going?"

Neil glanced at me before turning back to the stove. "It's going alright. We're trying to expand our territory to the north, but it's been a bit of a struggle. Other packs already have claims on the land we want, and we're trying to negotiate a deal that will benefit everyone. It's a delicate balance."

"I see," I said, fidgeting with my hands. "Do you think you'll be able to work it out?"

Neil shrugged. "It's hard to say. We're making progress, but it's slow going. We'll just have to see how things develop." He paused, looking over at me. "But enough about pack business. Let's talk about us."

I tensed up, knowing where this conversation was going. "Neil, I really don't think we would work out. I'm sorry if I gave you the wrong impression earlier, but I'm just not interested in pursuing anything with you."

Neil sighed, stirring the pasta. "I know you think that, Ella. But I know I can make you happy if you just give me a chance."

I shook my head. "I can't, Neil. I'm sorry. I just don't feel that way about you."

He turned off the stove abruptly. "Let's eat," he said. His voice was clipped and a little strained. I nodded and grabbed the plates, following him into the ornate dining room.

"Wine?" He held up a bottle and frowned when I shook my head.

"I don't drink," I explained. "But I don't mind if you do."

"Of course, you don't mind if I drink. Why would you?" Neil smirked. "And I'm sure your own tastes could change with time and influence."

"What did you end up making for us?" I asked, eager to change the subject. "It looks delicious."

Neil didn't answer. He took a long drink from his wineglass, studying me carefully.

"What are you looking forward to most, Ella? A mate who will give in to anything you say? Maybe he'll let you wear the pants and make all the decisions?"

I sighed. "No."

"Hmmm. I didn't think so." He served us both from the salad bowl and then piled some pasta on, too.

I took a bite, and my eyes widened. It was really good. Great, even.

"I think you missed your calling by becoming beta. You should have been a chef."

Neil chuckled. "Maybe in another life."

We ate in silence for a few minutes, the only sound coming from the clinking of our silverware against the plates. I couldn't help but feel like I was walking on eggshells around him. He seemed so unpredictable, like he could snap at any moment.

"So, how's the bakery doing?" he asked suddenly, breaking the silence, and catching me off guard. "You and Heather are joint owners, correct?"

"We are. And it's doing well," I said. "We're getting more and more customers every week, and I'm even thinking about expanding the menu."

Neil nodded. "That's great to hear. I'm glad you're finding success in something you're passionate about."

I smiled, feeling a little more relaxed. "Thanks. It's been a lot of hard work, but it's worth it."

We finished our meal without any more awkward moments, and I helped Neil clean up the dishes. As we were putting away the leftover food, Neil turned to me, his expression serious.

"Ella, I only want what's best for you. I understand that you have feelings for the omega. It's only natural, what with the true mate bond coloring your perception, but I think you're making a mistake by choosing him over me."

I shook my head, feeling exasperated. "Neil, you can't force someone to love you. It just doesn't work that way."

"Maybe. But I believe that if you gave me a chance and opened yourself up to the possibility of being with me, you would learn to love me."

I sighed, feeling tired. "Neil, I don't know what to say. I appreciate your honesty, but I just don't see us ever being together. Thanks for everything, but I think it's time for me to go."

I went to put on my jacket, but Neil grabbed my wrist before I could open the closet door.

"Ella, what am I going to do with you?"

I jumped, startled by how close he was. His face was

inches from my ear, causing his whisper to sound eerie. "What do you mean? Let go of me."

"I tried to let you come to the right conclusion on your own, but maybe you need a firmer hand. I can do that for you, Ella. I can just tell you what to think, how to act. Whatever you need, I'll provide it."

"What do you mean? I told you this wasn't what I wanted, and I meant it, Neil. If you don't want to drive me back to the bakery, that's fine. I'll just call someone else."

Neil spun me around so that we were facing each other and brushed a lock of hair from my face. His chuckle felt warm against my cheek. "Oh, Ella. You still don't get it. You won't leave this house until you have time to reconsider my generous offer. Don't worry. I can be a patient man, too."

Chapter 13

I shouldn't have come; that much was obvious. It was also becoming painfully clear why everyone had warned me about Neil in the first place. I hadn't listened, and now I was locked in one of the upstairs bedrooms trying to figure out what to do next.

Maybe I could shift and try to break down one of the doors? That might work, but I'd have to wait for him to leave in order to stand a chance at getting out of the house. With Jeremy "out of town," who knows how long I might be stuck in that room.

I cursed myself for asking Gabe to break our telepathic connection. I would've had to wait until one of us was asleep to use it, but it was better than nothing.

The thought caused a new idea to grow in my mind. Just because I knew the connection wouldn't work didn't mean Neil had to find out. The wheels in my head were still turning when I heard the key fit in the doorknob.

"Enjoying the room?" Neil smiled and greeted me as if we were on vacation together and he had just stepped outside to get some fresh air.

I snorted. "Do I even want to know why this room locks

from the outside? Have you kept other members of the pack locked away before?"

His face crumbled, and he grabbed his chest in exaggeration as though I had offended him. Clearly, I hadn't. "I had to switch the handle around before picking you up from work. I was hoping you'd listen to reason, and this wouldn't be necessary, but it's fine. I'll meet you where you are, Ella, and you just need a little time and encouragement."

The smile on his face didn't reach his cold eyes once again, and I was reminded of the times he had given me a similar look.

"You did something to my car. So I would have to spend time with you that night."

Neil shrugged. I'm guilty but charming, his upturned hands and smirk said. "You were going to put me off for a week or more. I needed to speed things up, Ella. Don't worry; you'll thank me later."

"What exactly is your plan here, Neil? Keep me locked up in this room until I change my mind? No way is Jeremy going to be cool with this when he gets back, and Heather knows I'm with you. If I don't show up to work tomorrow, she'll know something's wrong."

"Anything else? Or are you done?" Neil raised an eyebrow as though my words were boring him. This enraged and emboldened me. Time to go for the throat.

"Even though Gabe and I haven't completed the mating bond, we have started to see each other's thoughts and feel each other's feelings. He'll be able to tell where I am, and we can communicate even without my phone."

Neil sighed and pinched the bridge of his nose like he

was experiencing the start of a headache.

"If you don't believe me, ask Jeremy. Mariam started to experience the same thing when Trace was searching for her and—"

"Enough," he snapped. "I know all about that. You can see each other when one of you is asleep. It just means that I need to speed up the timeline a little bit, that's all."

I frowned. "What do you mean 'speed up the timeline'?"

"I told you I'd be patient, but it seems we don't have that luxury since you didn't follow my advice and break off that stupid bond earlier. It looks like we will need to break it before one of you decides to take a fucking nap."

He started loosening his tie and removing his suit jacket. I paled, the horror of what was going to happen washing over me.

"Are you saying…no, you can't be serious. What exactly do you think is going to happen here?"

Neil grimaced as he unbuttoned his shirt. "Given what he said the other night, I figured that just sleeping with you would be enough to get rid of him, and then we could wait until you were ready for the mating bite, but now I'm not going to risk it. We have to do this the right way and break the whole bond so he doesn't come sniffing around. So, Ella, I'm going to bite and claim you to fix this mess."

Heart pounding, I raced to the window and tried to pry it open. I banged on the glass and shouted, hoping that someone on the street below would hear me. But it was no use. Neil was too quick and caught me by the waist, yanking me away from the window. His cologne filled my nostrils, making me nauseous.

"Stop struggling. It's for your own good. You'll thank me

once it's done." His words were cold and calculated, and I knew then that he had no intention of letting me go.

I kicked and screamed, but his grip on me was too tight. His eyes dared me to continue, and I knew better than to provoke him any further.

Neil pulled me closer, his breath hot against my ear as he whispered, "Don't make this harder than it needs to be, Ella. Just submit."

His eyes flickered, the wolf inside trying to prevent the bite from happening. But it was useless; his human's desire to claim me was too strong.

I felt his sharp teeth sink into my neck, and a scream escaped my lips. It was painful but also pleasurable, sending my mind into overdrive. My body reacted against my will, and soon I found myself pressed against his hard body, arching my back to give him better access to my neck.

"That's a good girl," he crooned. His fingers trailed my back lightly, setting my skin on fire.

I knew I should fight it, but my body was betraying me, responding to his touch. It made me feel dirty like I was cheating on Gabe, even though I had no control over what was happening. My thoughts were jumbled, and I couldn't form a cohesive sentence.

I was left panting and confused as Neil pulled away from my neck. But then it was like a fog had lifted from my mind, and I could think clearly again.

"Now, that wasn't so bad, was it?" Neil chuckled, and I felt sick to my stomach. "And I'm about to make it feel even better, mate."

"What did you do to me?" I managed to ask, my voice

shaking.

"I've marked you as mine. It's what I needed to do to break the bond between you and that fucking omega. Once we mate, that bond will be severed, and you will belong to me." His eyes flashed with desire, and I found myself falling forward, desperate with need. Mariam had told me this would happen. With the mating bite comes insatiable lust.

My brain felt foggy once more, and it was difficult to concentrate, but I frowned at the sounds of banging and stomping that vibrated through the floorboards. It started below and moved up the stairs, ending with the door flying open and Gabe bursting into the room. His eyes were wild with rage as he took in the sight of Neil's near nudity and his hands on my body.

Gabe swore and lunged forward, grabbing Neil by his waist, and forcing him to the floor. Under normal circumstances, the beta would have had the upper hand, but Gabe seemed to have a boost of strength that made Neil no match for his aggression. His fist came down to Neil's face over and over again, causing blood to spread onto the carpet. I stared at them both in shock, struggling to comprehend what was happening. My wolf growled and whimpered. She was as distressed and confused as I was.

When Neil finally stopped moving, Gabe scooped me up and carried me into the hallway like I weighed nothing. He slammed the door shut behind us. It locked with a loud click.

It was a smart move; I could already hear Neil stirring on the other side.

Gabe held me close and bolted outside, going straight for my car.

He set me in the passenger's seat like he thought I could shatter at any moment. He buckled himself in, too, but didn't start driving right away. Instead, he leaned over and whispered soothing words into my ear, stroking my hair gently. Tears rolled down my cheeks, and my body trembled. Gabe gently traced his fingers over the fast-healing scar, causing intense pressure to shoot between my legs. The area was more sensitive than anything I had ever felt, and suddenly my only thought was how to get back in the house to complete the connection with Neil.

Gabe grabbed my wrist and locked the doors to keep me from going back into the house. He tried to soothe me and kept apologizing. "I should have known better than to leave you alone. I thought you would come by the hotel after work, but then Heather showed up. She was worried about you. I'm so sorry, Ella. I'm so sorry."

I didn't care that he was sorry. All I wanted to do was run back to Neil and tear my clothes off. "Please let me go," I begged him. "I need him. I have to go back."

He swallowed hard but kept his grip firm until he had my seatbelt fastened. Gabe started my car and pulled away from the alpha house, never taking one hand off my seatbelt buckle. I know because I did everything possible to pry it away from him and undo the restraint.

"It's going to be okay, Ella. Trust me. I know there's an answer to this somewhere in the library back home. I just need to get us to Tumblewild so I can find it."

My tears ran freely, but I stopped trying to get away. The car was moving too fast, and my wolf was no help. She was hiding somewhere in the shadows, trying to avoid getting involved at all. She just wanted this whole thing to be over.

"Please, Gabe. He bit me. I need him."

"I know, Ella. But you don't understand what you're saying. Give it an hour or two, and let's get some distance from him, and you'll change your mind." Gabe fumbled with my purse, his eyes still on the road. "Can you get me your phone? You have Jeremy's number, right?"

I nodded and curled up in the seat, my legs tucked under my chin. The sensitive place between my legs was throbbing, and it felt like there was nothing I could do to satisfy the ache. Still, I tried to rock against the heel of my shoe, praying that the friction would give me some relief.

Gabe glanced at me, his teeth already extended and eyes darkening.

"Ella, whatever you're doing over there, I need you to stop. The more… aroused you are, the harder it's going to be for me to concentrate on getting us home."

"I'm sorry," I whined. "It's just… I can't help it."

Gabe took a few deep breaths and used my phone to call Jeremy. He quickly explained what had happened with Neil and that we were headed to Tumblewild. Whatever Jeremy said in return didn't sit well with Gabe. He tried to argue but eventually sighed and handed me the phone.

"He wants to talk to you," he grumbled. "Feel free to hang up on him if you want."

I took the phone from Gabe, careful to avoid touching his hand. "Hello?"

"Ella, are you okay?" Jeremy's voice was deep on the other end. Pure alpha.

"I don't know," I said honestly. "I just want to go back to Neil. Gabe took me, and he's driving me to Tumblewild. I guess that's what I wanted, but now I'm not sure."

A loud crash came from his end. It sounded like he must have thrown something. "Listen, Ella, this isn't your fault. You're in a really compromised position after being bitten, and Gabe's trying to prevent you from being tied to that *motherfucker* permanently. It will be rough for a little while, but it will get easier the longer you're away from him. Just... hang tight with Gabe until he can fix this. I'm going home to deal with *Neil*."

The alpha spat out the name of his beta like it was leaving a bad taste in his mouth. I hung up, trying and failing to ignore the throbbing between my legs. Eventually, I was able to fall asleep and find some solace in being unconscious.

When I woke up, it was dark outside. The day's events had completely drained me, so I guess I shouldn't be surprised. At least the desperation I felt for Neil was beginning to subside. While my arousal felt uncomfortable, it wasn't unbearable anymore.

"Where are we?" I asked, sitting up in the passenger seat. It felt weird riding on this side of my car. I hadn't done that since my mom had driven it.

"Bakersfield," Gabe answered. He glanced at me, his expression tight. "Did the nap help?"

I nodded. "Yeah, I think so. My wolf is still really skittish."

It was true; the animal was still hiding, not sure what to feel or how to react. Having a mating bite forced upon you had that effect, I guess.

Gabe pulled into the parking lot of a budget hotel. It was right off the freeway and looked a little rundown, but it didn't matter. I glanced at the keys in his hand as he killed the engine.

He raised his eyebrows, hesitating. Always hesitating.

You know who never hesitates?

Neil.

I shook my head at the unwanted thought.

"I need to go inside to get us a room, but I don't think leaving you alone is a good idea. Come in with me?"

I scowled. "What? Do you think I'm going to try and run back to Dark Claw? Try and find Neil to complete the mating bond with him?"

Gabe shrugged. "I don't know. Are you?"

"No!" I said, feeling defensive and more than a little guilty. "Well…I don't think so." I slumped back in the seat.

Hey, it's okay," he said. He reached over to grab my hand, but I pulled away. The contact I had with him when he carried me out of the room was horrible and made me want to complete the bond even more. I wasn't willing to risk a reaction like that again.

Hurt flashed briefly on his face, but he hid it quickly. "Come on, Ella. Let's go and settle in for the night."

The hotel only had one room available, but that was fine. Gabe wasn't going to leave me on my own, anyway. We talked side-by-side until we found the door marked 'A3.' I wanted to take another shower, but neither of us had any clothes to change into. There hadn't been any time to pack. I guess Gabe had abandoned his stuff at the hotel back in Dark Claw.

"This is it," he said, running the card through the reader.

He pushed the door open, and we both groaned.

Of course, there was only one bed.

"I'll take the couch," he said. The room was outdated, with a lot of burgundy and gold everywhere. I waved away his offer.

"It's a king. We can both sleep on it and just make a mountain of pillows between us."

Gabe shrugged. "If you think you'll be alright, that's fine with me. Are you hungry?" He held up an assortment of takeout menus that had been placed next to the phone.

We ended up skipping the shower and ordering takeout from a Thai restaurant instead. He dove in as soon as it was delivered, making me feel a little guilty. I had eaten lunch with Neil but hadn't considered when he might have eaten last. I picked up my plate but didn't open it.

"What's wrong?" He shot me a concerned glance. "Do you regret not going for the squid?"

I rolled my eyes and cracked a grin. "You might be willing to try anything once, but not me."

I grabbed the remote and flipped through some of the channels. I didn't really care what we watched. Just having the background noise to help fill the silence was enough.

"Hey, you skipped past that one show with the people living in New York."

I looked at him, surprised. "You mean *Friends*?"

"Yeah, I watched one with Mariam, and it was pretty funny. Are you a mega fan like she is?"

"Hardly," I said. But I flipped back to the rerun and laughed with Gabe at the crew trying to move the couch. It felt nice to relax, and it seemed like he felt the same way.

Eventually, my eyes started drooping, and Gabe stifled a

few yawns.

"If we're going to get back on the road tomorrow, we should probably get ready for bed."

"Yeah, I guess so," I agreed. Neither of us moved. "I bet this wasn't what you had in mind for your first night with your true mate."

Gabe laughed bitterly. "You mean sleeping with a barrier between us and another man's mark on her neck. No, it wasn't. You've got me there, Ella."

I winced. It sounded even worse when he said it all out loud.

"Hey," Gabe said. He leaned closer, and for a second, I thought he was going to reach for my hand again, but he didn't. "We'll get through this. This isn't your fault, and we're going to find a way to remove his mark. But you have to admit, this is a little… unorthodox."

The corners of his mouth twitched, and I found myself grinning back because his smile was infectious. "Now that you mention it, I'm not sure we should even be alone in here together. My mom always said I should wait to spend the night with someone until we were mated."

"It's all very scandalous," he agreed with a straight face. "And I wouldn't want to speak for your mother, but she might make an exception. Just this once."

I shook my head and helped pile the pillows in the center of the bed. Gabe was asleep as soon as his body hit the mattress, leaving me alone to sneak off into the bathroom and inspect the mating bite on my neck. The freshly healed skin was pink and shiny, but the pain was gone. The physical pain, at least. The other kind, the worst kind of pain, was still hitting hard.

Chapter 14

The sunrise view of the city was breathtaking, and I decided to enjoy it with a cup of coffee out on the balcony. I smiled, thinking that Mariam would be shocked that I was drinking regular as I typically stuck to decaf. She might even be a little impressed that I was shaking things up.

Mariam. I frowned. I needed to call her or at least answer her texts. They had gone from concerned to annoyed and then back to concerned over the past few days. But if nothing else, I would see her in person soon enough.

Gabe had slept in. Not surprising, seeing as how he couldn't nap in the car, but I could finally hear him stirring in the hotel room. The rustling of the sheets was followed by a thud and several frantic footsteps. I raised my eyebrows and took a long drink from the paper hotel mug when the door flew open, revealing the panicked male shifter inside.

"You thought I left," It wasn't a question; his relief at seeing me planted firmly on the old wicker furniture confirmed it. "You slept hard last night. It wouldn't have been too difficult to give you the slip, you know."

Gabe snorted and ran his fingers through his sleep-tousled hair. "Yeah, I guess you could have. What with Pillow Mountain keeping us apart."

"Want some crappy coffee? There's enough in the pot for another cup."

His nostrils flared as he studied the brown sludge I was drinking. I sighed. "It won't win any awards, but the caffeine might help. We have another seven hours until we get to Tumblewild, right?"

Gabe groaned and nodded. "Don't remind me. Yeah, I guess I better have some, too, and then we can get going. I can't wait to shower and change into some clean clothes."

I laughed. "I can't wait for that either. You've seen better days."

He grabbed his chest, mimicking a broken heart. "Ouch. Add that to the list of things I didn't think my true mate would say after our first evening together."

I threw a tobacco-scented cushion at him.

Gabe caught it with ease and tossed it back at me. "You're lucky I like you," he said, grinning.

I leaned back in my chair, savoring the warmth of the sun on my face. It was a beautiful day, one that was meant to be enjoyed. Only one thing was stopping me from doing just that: Neil's mating mark on my neck. It was annoying, just distracting enough for me not to forget it was there.

"Penny for your thoughts," Gabe offered, returning with his own mug. He set it on the table between us and stretched out in the second old chair.

"Have you thought about what happens if we can't remove the mark?"

Gabe didn't answer right away. He blew on the coffee,

and we watched the steam circle in the morning air.

"Of course, I have," he said finally. "But we can't focus on that right now. We just have to think positively. Besides, Mariam asked me the same thing when she first received Trace's bite. You know, before she fell head over heels for him. I did a little digging for her back then, and I'm pretty sure there is something we can do about it. Fingers crossed, it's as easy as replacing his bite with mine."

I choked on the horrible coffee. The thought of another male biting me, even my true mate, felt confusing with the mating mark on me. But remembering how it felt, how cock hungry I had been...Gabe might not have been the one who had marked me, but as my true mate, I had been more than willing to throw myself at him in lieu of consummating the bond with Neil. My face burned all the way down to the roots of my hair.

"Are you okay?" Gabe asked, reaching toward me. His fingers grazed my arm, trying to help me but setting off a new wave of desire in me.

Heat raced through me, replacing my embarrassment with...something else. I jumped from the chair and raced into the hotel room. The door leading to the hallway was within reach when Gabe tackled me to the floor. His body covered me as I squirmed beneath him.

He held my hands firmly above my head, parting my legs with his knee. I felt his cock swell and nudge against me, lining up perfectly to fit inside. I writhed at the contact, hungry for more.

"Please, Gabe," I begged. "I need you. I need you."

"Fuck, Ella," he growled. "You don't know what it does to me when you talk like that."

Gabe fisted my hair with his free hand and brought my lips to meet him. Our hips moved in tandem with our mouths, pushing in and pulling away. I felt my wolf spilled out, her eyes shifting to over mine.

"Claim us, mate," she coaxed him. "Remove the mark from the imposter male."

Gabe's teeth elongated, and his kiss became more urgent. His thrusts against my core were hard enough to bruise, but I met his every stroke. If only I could get his pants off and remove the thin layers of fabric between us.

As if reading my mind, he released my hands and broke our kiss. I scrambled for his belt, but instead of allowing me access to his body, he pulled me to my feet and carried me to the bathroom. In one fluid motion, he set me inside and slammed the door shut.

"Gabe!" I shouted. It felt like the wind had been knocked out of me. I pounded on the door with my fists and tried to turn the handle, but he was holding it shut from the other side. "Let me out of here, you jerk!"

I kicked the door a few more times for good measure, but he wouldn't budge or even answer. I spun around, trying to find something, anything, that might help me escape. *If only there was a window I could crawl out of…*

I growled low in frustration.

Take over, I told my wolf as I stripped out of my clothes. Happy to oblige, she initiated the shift.

———

Gabe held the door shut while Ella raged at being locked in. It had taken every last ounce of his self-control not to rip her clothes off and take her right then on the floor. She had been so wet, so willing, and even now, her arousal clung to their air.

That, and her anger.

It was actually his wolf who had stopped him. Some might call his wolf the wild animal, but the creature's only goal was to protect and care for their mate. Somewhere, deep inside, the wolf knew why Gabe was hesitant to bite Ella and claim her for them, and in the end, the animal was the only thing strong enough to prevent the man from fucking everything up and endangering Ella.

He had also been wary of Samantha and her endless flirting, so maybe Gabe owed him a little more credit than he usually got for that reason, too.

The pounding on the door had stopped, and now it was suspiciously quiet. Gabe's wolf tensed and then yipped like a pup. He had to smile at the animal's antics.

"Ella? Are you alright?" No answer. "Okay…I'm going to open the door. Please don't try to bum-rush me or anything."

Gabe eased the door open and was greeted by her wolf. She was beautiful, exactly how he remembered her from their run in the woods.

"Hey, girl. Your human is having a hard time, but you're helping her, aren't you?"

He ran his hands through her thick fur. Unlike Ella, she leaned into his touch, happy for the connection. Normally after a mating bite, the female shifter would experience intense feelings of arousal, but only for the one who gave them the mark. Ella's situation was a little different because the one who bit her wasn't a true mate. And yeah, chosen matings happened a lot, and that alone shouldn't be a problem, but since the bond wasn't completed and her true mate was in her direct proximity afterward, the waters were muddled.

If nothing else, their situation would make for interesting casework for the pack historian. *Future generations will be reading about this for years.*

Ella wanted Neil, but she wanted Gabe, too, and that hurt like hell. But he needed to be strong and shelve those feelings. *If- no, when- I figure out how to remove Neil's claim, Ella's attention will be all mine, and she'll hunger for my hands on her body*, he promised himself.

His wolf howled. He agreed wholeheartedly with that plan.

For now, scratching her beautiful wolf behind the ears would have to be enough.

"You're a good girl," Gabe whispered.

Her tongue lolled out one side of her mouth, giving the distinct impersonation of a grin. Gabe walked into the bathroom and collected Ella's discarded clothes. They weren't torn, so her wolf hadn't forced a shift. Maybe Ella needed to stay in this form. Maybe it was making things easier for her.

He took one last drink from the now-cold coffee cup and led the large she-wolf outside.

"Come on, let's get back to Flagstaff. We still have a long drive ahead of us," Gabe said. "Hopefully, anyone who sees you thinks you're just an oversized house pet."

He opened the car door, and the large wolf leaped inside, happy to be out of the oppressive motel room. He started up the engine, and they hit the road. The sun was high in the sky, beating down on the desert landscape as they drove on the highway past smaller towns.

They stopped a few times at a deserted exit to let his mate stretch her legs. Gabe was nervous when she didn't want to return to the car right away.

"We've got to leave," he pleaded. "We're still a few hours from home, Ella, and I want to start researching before the library closes."

Sensing his distress, she trotted back to the car without further complaint. His mate was much more compliant in this form, it seemed. As a wolf, she could be free without the worries and restrictions that she usually placed upon herself. She didn't have to be the responsible one, for once. She let Gabe take care of all that.

In return, his wolf's dominant nature was peaking. The creature was smitten with her creature, just as Gabe was with the woman herself. The moon goddess had definitely not made a mistake. Hopefully, Ella would come to feel the same way.

The final leg of the trip was the longest, but at last, they were driving through the streets of Flagstaff, mere miles away from the Tumblewild pack lands. Gabe silently debated whether he should take Ella's wolf back to his apartment. If she remained as a wolf, she would probably be most comfortable there, but he was worried that her human might try and force a shift. The Ella at the motel was ready to run away in search of Neil, and even now, Gabe couldn't be sure this Ella wouldn't try something like that.

After weighing all the options, he decided to bring her to the alpha's house. Trace had the resources to keep her safe while he conducted the necessary research, and the space was already familiar to her. It was the most logical solution to a variety of complications.

The drive to the alpha house had him feeling slightly nostalgic as he remembered the night of their first date. "I'm not as frustrated with you this time," Gabe said to the wolf beside him. "Although that can change quickly if you try to give me the slip again."

Her ears twitched in response as though she understood each word.

Gabe slowed to turn into the long driveway, knowing that his mate would be happy to get out of the car. She was more than a little charming, scenting the air with her nose upturned in the wind. Mariam met them at the door, welcoming her sister's wolf and her human mate without batting an eyelash. Gabe had called her a few times on the road when Ella was napping the night before to explain what had happened in Dark Claw.

Now, hours later, he followed the large she-wolf up the front steps, stopping just short of entering the home. As much as he wanted to relax after the long drive, there were other things he needed to do.

"If she decides to shift before I get back, she'll need these." Gabe handed Ella's clothes to her sister. "Fair warning, the whole mess with Neil has her jumpy. She tried to get away from me earlier, probably to go find him."

Mariam gave him a sympathetic look. "That had to be difficult for you."

Gabe shrugged, not wanting to let on how much the situation still stung. "I'll just be glad when this is all over and Ella's mine." Her wolf nudged his hand in agreement.

"Don't worry about anything. After you called, Trace sent

over some extra council members to help keep the place secure. Although, I think he was more concerned with Neil trying to get in than with Ella looking to get out," she said, her tone turning somber. "Neil was always an asshole, but I never thought he would do anything like this. I guess we should all pay more attention to those gut feelings that something's wrong, you know?"

Yeah, I knew all about that. If I had just told Ella to stay away from him or insisted on picking her up from work, none of this would have happened."

Mariam shook her head. "You're assuming she would have listened to you, which isn't a guarantee."

Gabe had to admit, she was right about that. And if he didn't know better, he would have sworn Ella's wolf looked a little guilty. She licked his hand and trotted away, leaving him to do what he must.

He said goodbye to Mariam, praying to the goddess that nothing would go wrong while he was gone. The only nice part about leaving in his mate's car was getting to enjoy her scent that lingered inside. Gabe inhaled deeply, trusting that she would be waiting for him when he got back.

He would have to be quick if he wanted to do any meaningful research before closing time. To the average human, the library looked nondescript, with a circulation desk that housed a kind older librarian who just happened to be one of Gabe's favorite members of the Tumblewild pack. He nodded to Ms. Lewis as he walked toward the inconspicuous side door that led to a room filled with werewolf books and scrolls. The recent annuals of pack and werewolf law gleamed, but many of the editions had been untouched for years. The musty smell of aged paper filled his senses, and he immediately felt the same overwhelming sense of awe he always did when looking upon the vast collection.

Gabe combed through the stacks, pulling out books written by master shifters on topics like advanced mating rituals, ancient remedies, and more. Ella's situation was complicated—but not impossible, he told himself— so it would probably take me hours, if not days, to find something, anything that could help us.

When night fell, and Ms. Lewis came to lock the library doors, he was still no closer to finding an answer than when he started. Gabe thought back on the days leading up to this one and how it was basically a rivalry between two males over the same female. He had spent most of his time looking at herbal remedies, hoping some potion could dissolve the mating bite, but maybe he should try to find information on how werewolf packs had originally split apart. Maybe one of them had dissolved over a disagreement between a chosen versus a true mate.

His wolf was itching to break free and run back to their mate at the alpha's house, but Gabe refused to hand over control. Right now, all he wanted was to make sure Ella was still safe, have a shower, and eat a good meal. In that order, specifically. He was too drained emotionally to go for a run and delaying how quickly they would get there was out of the question. So, back in the car he went.

"She's resting," Mariam said when she met Gabe at the front door. "She ate and took a bath. I think she's feeling better, but she didn't want to talk about it. I think she's, you know... a little embarrassed about the whole thing."

Gabe scowled. "She doesn't have anything to be embarrassed over. The beta had everyone, even his own alpha, believing that he wasn't a horrible person. There's no way she could have known he would try to force a mating bond with her."

"I know that, and you know that, but Ella has always been really hard on herself. Add that to the fact that she's still drawn to that prick, and you have the perfect storm for her to feel like shit."

"You always did have a way with words, mate." Mariam and Gabe glanced into the foyer where Trace was waiting for us. "Are you going to invite him inside, or are we keeping our guests on the front porch these days?"

Mariam stuck out her tongue at the alpha's teasing, earning her a raised eyebrow. Trace's reaction was enough to settle her feistiness. As bold as Mariam was, there was never a question of who was in charge.

Maybe someday that will be Ella and me, Gabe thought.

His wolf perked up. He had been pouting over being denied his run, but the idea of dominating Ella was compelling enough to draw his interest.

Easy, Gabe warned him. *We have to get her to accept our bond first. And before that can happen, we have to remove the claim that Neil left.*

Gabe followed Mariam up the stairs to the room Ella had stayed in for her mating ceremony. He froze, realizing how recent that was.

"Did all of this interrupt your vacation, Mariam? I know you planned on getting away with Trace after the ceremony."

She waved away his concern. "We cut it short. I'd rather

be here for you and my sister right now, anyway. We can go on vacation another time."

"You're a good friend, Mare. And an even better sister."

Mariam wrapped her arms around Gabe, giving him a tight hug. "You were there for me when no one else was. You let me stay in your apartment, for fuck's sake. And Ella practically raised me, and that was *not* an easy undertaking."

"Somehow, I believe that," he joked. "Teenage Mariam must have been hell on wheels."

She released Gabe quickly with a growl that turned into a guilty smile.

"Can Ella stay here with you?" he asked. "I would love to bring her back to my apartment, but until I know what we need to do to break Neil's claim, I'm afraid to…well, you know…."

His whole face heated as he tried to stammer through his concern over being intimate with Ella too soon.

"Of course," Mariam said gently. "But you should probably be the one to explain that to her. The Ella I know would rather gouge her eyes out over talking to me about her sex life. Even if it is a hypothetical sex life at this point."

She gave Gabe's arm one more squeeze and left him in the hallway at the same door that had held the mysterious scent on the day he first met Ella. At least this time, Gabe could figure out how to use the handle instead of breaking the whole thing down.

"Ella? Are you awake?" The room was dark, but Gabe could make out her human form under the covers on the bed.

She stirred and turned toward him. "Come to bed, Gabe. I'm tired."

His mouth went dry at her invitation. "Ella," he croaked. "I'm going back to my apartment until this thing with Neil is sorted out. It's for the best."

He didn't wait for a response. He needed to get out of that room. If she invited him into the bed with her again, there was a really good chance he wouldn't be able to say no.

Chapter 15

I stayed in the darkness for a long time, fully awake and feeling the sting of Gabe's abrupt departure. I wasn't trying to seduce him. I'd just wanted to have him in the room, even if we needed a mountain of pillows as a barrier again. Somehow having another person around helped a lot, especially someone with his soothing presence, but he couldn't stand to be with me even for that.

And was it my imagination, or was there a bitterness in his voice when he choked out his hasty goodbye? The way he implied all this was my problem to resolve made it pretty clear that he was getting fed up with my compulsive infatuation with Neil. And who could blame him? It had to be a new and fresh hell to be reminded that your true mate wanted sex with another male over and over again.

If only I had stayed in Tumblewild and given Gabe a chance after the mating ceremony, none of this would have happened. Sure, maybe we would've discovered that we were ultimately a bad fit, or maybe I would've just grown up and accepted that we could have a good relationship without him being dominant or having a werewolf-level build. Instead, I had chosen to take my chances with Neil. I groaned into the pillow, feeling like a total idiot.

Deep down, I knew his actions weren't my fault, but I was the one who had ignored everyone's warnings about him. I shuddered, imagining Justine having to fight him off, too. If only I had been as strong as she was, I wouldn't have his bite on my neck.

Nope. Stop that thinking. I wasn't going to victim-blame myself anymore. I couldn't change what happened, but it wasn't my fault and I'd find some way to make the future better for myself.

Broken down and tired, I curled up into a tight ball and tried to will away the tears when they spilled from my eyes. Eventually, they must have stopped falling, but only after I was sleeping too deeply to notice.

The next morning, I got up slowly, trying to shake off the hurt from the night before. I needed to pull myself together, at least enough to face Mariam and Trace at breakfast.

I dressed and put on a little makeup to hide my puffy eyes before heading downstairs. A warm breeze blew in through an open window in the living room, carrying with it notes of wildflowers from outside. I breathed deeply, allowing the scent to work its soothing magic on me.

Mariam and Trace were already seated at the table when I entered; their conversation paused momentarily as they acknowledged my presence. Mariam gave me a sympathetic smile and motioned for me to sit next to her.

"Good morning, Ella," she said softly. "How are you feeling today?"

I shrugged, not quite sure how to respond. "Better, I guess. It's just a lot to process."

Trace cleared his throat, breaking the awkward silence. "We were thinking of taking a run through the woods today. Maybe a little exercise will do us all some good."

I nodded, grateful for the distraction and a little surprised that he would be joining us. Jeremy never seemed to have time for a random run in the woods. Or maybe Dark Claw's alpha could go for a run, and just didn't prioritize such things. "That sounds nice."

We finished our breakfast quickly and set out into the vast backyard, following a well-worn path that led us deeper into the heart of the forest. The further we went, the more I felt my tension melting away. The trees were tall and imposing, casting dappled shadows on the forest floor, and the air was cool and fresh.

We walked in comfortable silence for a while, the only sound coming from the crunch of leaves and twigs under our feet. Mariam and Trace kept a small distance from me, so I was able to enjoy the scenery without any distracting conversations.

As we walked, I couldn't help but think about Gabe. What would he be doing right now? Was he thinking about me? I shook my head, trying to push those thoughts aside. He was the last thing I needed to be thinking about.

Suddenly, Trace stopped in his tracks, his nostrils flaring as he sniffed the air. "Do you smell that?" he asked with a hint of excitement.

Mariam and I exchanged a confused look, but before we could ask, Trace took off running, shedding his clothes as he went. His wolf form tore through the underbrush, leaving us behind. Mariam and I followed although we took the time to set our clothing down in folded piles. Our own wolves were eager to see what all the excitement was about.

As we rounded a bend in the trail, we saw that Trace had taken off after a rabbit. Mariam and I didn't get the opportunity to hunt very often growing up in urban California. My wolf was savoring getting to hunt in such an unrestricted place, and I knew Mariam must be feeling the same way. For the first time, it was like the two of us were friends rather than polar opposites. We had a camaraderie in the woods. I allowed myself to savor the thrill of the run. I couldn't help but wonder if this was how it would be if things worked out with Gabe and I moved to Tumblewild permanently. Maybe this was exactly what I needed.

When we were too tired to run anymore, Mariam and I collapsed in the tall grass near the creek that ran through the alpha house property. Trace joined us sans rabbit. The hulking black wolf made for an intimidating predator, but I had to wonder if he let the animal go. For some shifters, it was more about the chase. All of his prowess melted away as he snuggled up next to his mate. She yawned and stretched, making room for him to join us in our bout of laziness.

The sun was high above us when we trotted back to our discarded clothes. Trace had to spend some time collecting his, and he was teased mercilessly for walking around in his underwear.

"At least it's a good view," Mariam giggled.

"I should probably go back to the house and call Gabe," I said. "Maybe he's found something useful at the library."

"If anyone could, it would be him," she agreed. "You

know that's where we first met, right? I had just arrived at Tumblewild and was trying to find a way out of mating with Trace. Gabe helped me navigate all those dusty old books because he was there researching something for the council. I knew he was a kindred spirit when he treated the materials so well. Most male werewolves wouldn't be interested in such things."

"He's very unique," I agreed.

"Does that mean you're going to give him a chance?" Mariam asked. "I think you should if I haven't made that clear already."

I smiled at her sadly. "I wouldn't get your hopes up." After he practically ran out of my room last night, neither of us should look too much into him researching a cure for me. Gabe was a good guy. He'd try to help even if he wasn't interested in pursuing our mating bond.

Mariam looked like she wanted to argue the point, but her attention was diverted by Trace walking towards us without a shirt. He grabbed her roughly by the waist and hauled her to him, causing her to laugh and squeal with delight. I rolled my eyes and looked away. Seeing them like this wasn't as painful as I thought it would be, but I still didn't need a front-row seat to their lovefest.

Trace's phone vibrated, and he gave Mariam a sheepish look.

"Go," she said, rubbing his chest and kissing him on the cheek. "Duty calls, and Randy's probably wondering if you're showing up at the office at all today."

"I was just saying that I need to go and check on Gabe at the library, too," I offered. "Is there a car I can borrow? He took mine with him last night, I think."

Trace nodded. "You can take Mariam's, or I can ask one of the guys to drive you if you want. That way, Gabe can drive you both home afterward. I'm sure he wouldn't mind a little extra quality time with his mate."

"Yeah, thanks. Sounds good." I didn't feel like arguing about Gabe's intentions anymore, especially not with Trace. He might be my brother-in-law, but he was also a bit bullheaded. I remembered clearly how difficult it was to convince him of anything when he raided my house in search of Mariam.

Trace left in a hurry with the promise that a young council member named Jared would by shortly to bring me to the library. I told him there was no rush; I was more than a little grateful for the chance to clean up after the run.

Thirty minutes later, I was freshly showered, changed into a new outfit from Mariam's closet, and ready to go. I realized too late that I had left my purse in the car, along with my phone and wallet. I made a mental note to grab those things ASAP.

"Ready?" Jared held open the door of the lifted truck for me. I should be used to the types of massive vehicles that shifter men seemed to prefer driving, but it took me a minute to hoist myself into the passenger seat nonetheless. Unfortunately, this one was also black and reminded me of Neil's truck.

"Let me guess. This is your gas saver, right?"

Jared chuckled and buckled his seatbelt. "It's a hybrid if that's what you mean. Trace is big on helping the environment."

I had meant the little jab as a joke, but that piece of information was good to know. I doubted Neil gave any consideration to the emissions coming out of his truck. My respect for Trace went up a few notches.

"So, how long have you been on the council, Jared?" I asked. "Do you usually get stuck driving people around for Trace?"

"Not long," he admitted. "But I don't mind running errands and helping out. Everyone on the council pitches in."

Interesting. From the grumblings I had heard, Jeremy usually left jobs like this to the newbies. But maybe spreading the chores around helped with morale. "Do you have a mate?"

His ears reddened a little, and he shook his head, eyes on the road. "No, ma'am. I'm still waiting for my true mate. A lot of us are, actually. I guess taking chosen mates have kind of gone out of style." He glanced at the scar on my neck, eyes wide as he realized his faux pas. "I mean, that's not to say taking a chosen mate is bad. It's complicated, of course."

"It's fine," I said, tugging on the collar of my shirt and wishing I had worn a turtleneck. "This wasn't exactly my idea, either."

"Yeah, I heard a little about what happened. That was pretty shitty. I'm sorry."

I stifled a groan. He knew about what happened with Neil? Was everyone in the pack talking about me?

"That was a stupid thing to say. Sorry. It's not like that, I promise," Jared said as if he could read my mind. "Gabe and I are close. We were friends in school, and we work together for the council. He'll probably be the next one appointed as soon as there's an opening, by the way. All that to say... most of the pack has no idea about what's going on. Gabe only told me some of it because he wanted me to handle his projects while he took some time off."

"It's fine," I said again, though the thought of Gabe talking to anyone about my situation with Neil felt violating. Jared seemed nice enough, but I didn't know him at all.

We arrived at the library without any other awkwardness, and I thanked him again for the ride.

Inside, I was greeted by the librarian and her young assistant, who reminded me of Mariam. My sister had a lot of interests, but she loved to read and had worked at the pack library when she lived at Dark Claw. It had been her go-to place to escape, similar to how my bakery was for me when I opened it with Heather. I should have figured this would be one of the first places she would visit after arriving in town.

"I'm looking for Gabe. Is he here?" I asked.

"You must be Ella. It's so good to meet you," the librarian stood and walked around the large circulation desk. I tried not to stiffen as she hugged me, and I managed to pat her gently on the back in return. "Gabe's where he normally is, right through there."

She pointed to a nondescript door, one that I was guessing led to the shifter collections. I thanked her and let myself in.

"Gabe? Are you in here?" The room was filled with books, and although I couldn't see him from the doorway, chances were he was somewhere in the maze of shelving.

"Ella?" His voice was a little muffled, but I was able to

teeter around the cramped room until I found him. He was sitting crisscrossed on the floor, surrounded by stacks of old editions of werewolf lore. His face brightened when he saw me at first, but then he seemed a little nervous. "How are you feeling?"

For a second, I thought maybe he was talking about last night, but then I realized he was referring to my episode at the hotel. "Don't worry. I won't make you have sex with me or anything."

Gabe gave me a strange look and gave a stiff laugh. "Good to know," he said.

I picked up one of the volumes that were resting on top of a nearby stack and traced the embossed gold letters with my finger.

"Tumblewild sure has a lot of old books. I wonder if Dark Claw has anything like this in our library. I'm ashamed to say I've never thought to look in our archives."

"According to Mariam, Dark Claw has a pretty good collection, too, but nothing like what we have when it comes to scrolls." He sighed and massaged his forehead like he felt a headache coming on. "Unfortunately, we might have to try and search through some of those, too. I'm not having any luck with these newer editions. The only problem is that the scrolls aren't organized very well... and a good portion of them aren't even written in English."

I set the book down. "Well, we have to start somewhere. What can I do to help?"

Gabe looked up at me with a mix of gratitude and hesitation. "Honestly, I don't know if I should even ask. You've already been through so much with Neil. I understand if you just need some down time."

I frowned at him. "You're doing this for me, Gabe, remember? So I won't stay tied to a psychopath? Just tell me what to do, and I'll do it."

He sighed and leaned back against the wall. "Okay. I'll take all the help I can get. Here, let me show you what I've found so far."

We spent the next few hours poring over ancient texts, trying to decipher the meaning behind the cryptic passages and piecing together clues as to what some of the old werewolf languages could mean. Gabe wasn't joking when he said the scrolls were disorganized. Potions were mixed in with philosophy and pack organization theory. It was tedious work, but I found myself getting lost in the process of discovery. Gabe was a patient teacher, explaining the intricacies of shifter history and mythology in a way that was easy to understand.

But as the sun started to set, I realized we hadn't made much progress. "I think I need a break," I said, rubbing my eyes. "It's getting late, and my brain is fried. Plus, I don't know about you, but I'm starving."

Gabe nodded, setting his scroll down. "Yeah, we've hit a wall for today. Let's call it a night and pick up where we left off tomorrow. Although, I might ask to take a few of these to look at later this evening. Check-out privileges are one of the perks of working for the council, I guess."

I stood up and stretched, feeling the kinks in my back pop. "Thanks, Gabe. I really... appreciate all your help."

"Of course, Ella. We'll figure this out together."

We headed out of the library, feeling a sense of accomplishment despite our lack of progress. At least I was doing something, anything, to take my mind off of Neil and my situation. And maybe, just maybe, we were getting closer to finding a solution.

We walked to my car, bodies close and hands just shy of touching. I felt an odd compulsion to reach for him, but last night he made it clear that he wasn't interested in getting closer, and I didn't want to risk setting off my baser instincts that the mating bite had unleashed. I could still feel it, of course, but the throbbing in my lower regions had abated enough that I could think and concentrate on other matters, like where we were going to eat, for instance.

"What do you feel like?" I asked. Gabe still had my keys, and he held open the passenger door for me, so I took that as a hint he wanted to drive.

"Not sure. Probably not the diner, though. I'm not ready to deal with all that at the moment."

Right, I thought. *Samantha.* It's crazy how easily she had slipped my mind.

"Would you want to…" Gabe hesitated. "Would you feel comfortable coming back to my place, and I could cook for you?"

I laughed. "Yes, I'm comfortable going back to your apartment, Gabe. But only on one condition."

He raised his eyebrows, waiting for the stipulation.

"I'm going to cook for you."

"Even better." He grinned, throwing the car in reverse, and taking us away from the small downtown.

His apartment was located in a pretty large development. At least, it was bigger than any that we had back home.

"This is it," Gabe said, opening the door with flair.

"Nothing too fancy, but I harbored your sister here like a fugitive for a whole month at one point."

I laughed and shook my head, going straight for the kitchen. "Okay, so what ingredients do you have to work with?"

"We're in luck because I think Jared dropped by some food when I told him I was coming back into town."

"That's not all you told him," I murmured under my breath.

Gabe froze. "Yeah, I did tell him about some of the things that are happening with us. I wanted him to understand that I wouldn't be coming back in to work anytime soon, but afterward, I was worried that maybe I shouldn't have said anything. Pack members in Tumblewild are not exactly known for their discretion if you catch my drift. I'm guessing he said something to you?"

"He let it slip when he drove me to the library. It's alright. I can understand why you told him. I'm just usually a pretty private person. Outside of Mariam and Heather, I don't share a lot about myself with anyone, and even those two don't know most things about me."

"Yeah, I have gotten the impression that you like to keep a lot of things bottled up," he said. "Maybe one day I'll be someone else you can open up to."

I frowned, not sure what he meant by that. My expression seemed to encourage him to change the subject.

He opened the fridge and checked the pantry, giving a satisfied nod. "There's a pretty good variety of staple items in here. Pasta, chicken, beef, tofu. I'm not picky, so whatever you feel like making is good with me."

"Are you leaving?" I asked.

"Actually, I was going to look over the scrolls I borrowed from the library. It might be a long shot, but I think they discuss some of the old mating laws that might help us out. Do you mind if I go and set them up in the living room?"

I shook my head. "Of course not. Let me know if you find something interesting."

"Ella. I guarantee you'll find out right away if I find anything useful at all," he teased.

I shooed him out of the kitchen and tied his apron around my waist. I was in the mood for something rich and filling. Luckily Gabe had all the ingredients for a garlic mushroom Bolognese.

I hummed to myself as I boiled the water and prepped my vegetables, enjoying the easy rhythm of being back in a kitchen. As I waited for the pasta to finish cooking, I scavenged some dark cocoa and sugar to make brownies for dessert.

I turned off the burners and was starting to plate the meal when Gabe appeared again.

"Hey, I was going to come and serve you. It was supposed to be a surprise," I chided. But when I looked over and saw the expression on his face, my smile disappeared. "What is it, Gabe? Did you find something?"

"I did. At least, I'm pretty sure I did. Don't worry, it's good news…at least, I think it's good news."

I waited for him to continue. Whatever it was had him pretty shaken up.

He took a deep breath. "The bite from Neil should be reversible, but it's going to take a few days. We have to wait until the next full moon… and you'll need to have it replaced with another mating mark."

I chewed on my bottom lip. That did complicate things, especially since I wasn't really sure where Gabe stood on the issue. But for some reason, he still seemed a little uncomfortable.

"That's not all," he said. "In order for the mark to take, the bite will have to be binding."

I blinked, not sure what he meant by that.

"Ella, the mating bond is two-fold. It doesn't matter what order it happens in usually, but in your case, I guess it does. In order for this to work, you'll need a mating bite on the night of the full moon, but before that, you'll have to complete the other part of the bond."

I felt my mouth go dry. Sex. He meant I would need to have sex before the next full moon.

Chapter 16

"I'll take these to one of the pack's historians tomorrow to make sure I'm not misunderstanding anything, but it seems pretty clear. I'm sorry, Ella. I'm not sure if you're ready for that, but at least we know his mark can be removed… or, more accurately, that it can be replaced."

I nodded and turned back to the food I was dishing. Suddenly I wasn't very hungry anymore.

Gabe's words hung heavy in the air between us. I tried to push them to the back of my mind as we ate, but it was impossible to think of anything else. What if he didn't want to have sex with me? Would I have to find someone else? Or would it be better to just remain partially tied to Neil forever?

After dinner, I excused myself to the bathroom, needing some space to think. I splashed cold water on my face, trying to calm myself down. It wasn't just the idea of having sex with Gabe that had me on edge, but the idea of being bound to him for the rest of my life. He had shut me down just last night for sex, and now everything would need to happen so soon! The next full moon was only a few days away. Maybe I could wait until another moon cycle to make a decision.

When I returned to the living room, Gabe was sitting on the couch, a stack of old scrolls in front of him. He looked up as I entered, his eyes locking onto mine.

"I'm sorry, Ella," he said softly. "I didn't mean to overwhelm you. I just want you to know I'll be here for you, no matter what you decide. We can figure this out together."

I nodded, not sure what else to say.

He gestured to the scrolls. "I didn't find much else, but I did come across an old ritual that might help with the reversing process. It involves taking a bath with herbs and oils after the unwanted mating bite, and I thought it might be something we could try."

I raised an eyebrow. "A bath ritual? That sounds... weird."

Gabe grinned. "Yeah, it's not exactly something I've ever done before, and it might be completely useless, but it's worth a shot, right? It's said to help cleanse the body and soul, and it might help break Neil's bond."

I considered his proposal for a moment, then nodded. "Okay, let's do it. It can't hurt to try."

We spent the next hour gathering the ingredients we needed for the bath. It felt like we emptied half of Gabe's spice rack, and it made me wonder if we were actually making some kind of disgusting soup instead.

Preparing for the ritual with Gabe felt oddly intimate. There was a certain closeness in how we moved together and how our hands brushed against each other. It was both terrifying and exhilarating.

Once the bath was ready and Gabe was standing firmly

outside the bathroom door, I slipped into the warm water. The smell of the herbs and oils washed over me, which wasn't entirely unpleasant.

"I'm in," I called out to him when I had the shower curtain rearranged to block my nudity.

If Gabe thought my modesty was strange given our circumstances, he didn't let on.

"How do you feel?" he asked.

I took a deep breath, trying to process the sensations flooding through me. "I don't know...it feels like I'm in a tub filled with oregano and chopped onions."

"Fair enough," he said, smiling.

I settled deeper into the water, letting the odd mixture of scents and heat soak into my skin. Gabe sat on the closed toilet seat, his eyes never leaving my face. There was something about the way he was looking at me that created a needy pulling sensation down below my belly. The shower curtain was hiding all the interesting parts of my body from view, and yet, it felt like I was on full display.

One thing was for sure: no one had ever gazed at me with that kind of intensity before. My stomach flip-flopped, not hating the idea of showing him a little bit more.

Where the heck did that idea come from?

Gabe cleared his throat. "Ella, do you trust me?"

His question caught me off guard. "Of course, I do. Without you, I'd be stuck in the worst mating bond of all time."

He hesitated, and I could tell he was debating whether to continue or not. "No, I mean... and maybe 'trust' isn't the right word here, but I know something is preventing you from wanting to be with me, Ella. I'm in this 100 percent, but Neil said something to me that has me wondering about you. About your needs, more specifically."

I stilled. "Neil talked to you? When? At my house?"

Gabe shook his head. "No, we had dinner together the night I stayed at the hotel. If you could call it dinner," he scoffed. "Neil was going on about your needs and how he could fulfill them in ways I couldn't, probably because I'm an omega. Is that how you feel, too?"

I averted my gaze to the tile floor, not sure how to answer. "Real talk, Gabe? I've been guilty of trying to plan my whole life around a fictional mate showing up and being a stereotypical tough guy. I can't deny that a part of Neil fit that picture, but no way is that option anymore."

"I didn't think so," he said. "But this isn't a competition between him and me, Ella. It's about whether you think I can give you what you need. I think I can. In fact, you probably are making incorrect judgments about me based on your beliefs about omegas. Like, that we don't discipline our mates or that we are submissive, too. Is that what's happening?"

"I... well, I mean, I don't know about all omegas, but you're pretty laid back, Gabe. I honestly can't imagine submitting to you," I answered. "I can see why Mariam says you're her best friend and that you're so nurturing. You are probably the nicest person I've ever met."

Gabe moved closer to the tub, his hand brushing against my arm. "I'm not Neil, Ella. And I'm not your dad or Trace. I'll never want to be an alpha or beta or even just a typical pack member. I like helping out the pack, and being an omega comes naturally to me, but that doesn't have anything to do with us."

"I'm not sure I understand," I admitted with a frown.

"Don't worry," he said. He leaned down so close that I thought he was going to kiss me. Instead, he stopped short, his words tickling my cheek. "Before the next full moon, I intend to show you."

The best part of the bath was when it was over, and I got to shower and rinse all the random grossness out of my hair. I had to submerge completely three times before clawing my way out of the basin. Gabe had graciously left the room when I asked, and now I was alone, trying to determine which bottle of his shampoo would be least likely to give me dandruff.

It was getting late, and I felt myself growing tired. As I was lathering up my hair, I heard a knock on the bathroom door.

"Ella, can I come back in?" Gabe asked tentatively.

I quickly rinsed out the shampoo and turned off the water. "Sure," I called out, wrapping a towel around myself as I stepped out of the shower.

Gabe opened the door and handed me some sweats and a tank top. They weren't mine, but I was surprised to find they were the correct size. He turned, giving me more privacy to shimmy into them.

"I picked up a few things after meeting you that first night at the alpha house," he explained. I felt myself blush at the thoughtfulness of the gesture. Though I suppose it could also be viewed as being presumptive that I would be moving in with him or something.

"You can stay here tonight," he said, gesturing down the hall to the bedroom. "I'll take the couch."

I shook my head. "Gabe, you don't have to do that. My car's here so I can just go to Mariam's. I'll call you in the morning."

Before I could move past him, Gabe placed a gentle hand on my shoulder. His voice was low and soft, but there was a steely determination beneath the surface. "No, Ella. You're staying here tonight."

I looked up at him, meeting his gaze head-on. There was an intensity in his eyes that took me aback. At that moment, I realized maybe there was more to Gabe than I had given him credit for.

"That sounds like an order, not a request."

He nodded slowly as his smile grew. "It was supposed to. I regretted leaving you alone last night. You belong in my bed, no exceptions."

My heart thudded hard at the confidence behind his words. Was it just me, or had something shifted between us?

I couldn't put my finger on it exactly, but there was something in the way his hand found the small of my back and firmly led me to the bedroom that made me weak at the knees. It had me conjuring up all kinds of sexy scenarios where he would be guiding me down this same hallway and into his bed.

As we entered the bedroom, Gabe dimmed the lights and lit a few candles. The smell of vanilla filled the air, enveloping me in a sense of comfort that I hadn't felt in a long time. It complemented his own sweet scent really well. The room was simple but cozy, with a queen-sized bed against the wall and a wooden dresser opposite it.

Just looking at the plush bedding made my eyes heavy.

Gabe gave me a small smile. "Get some rest, Ella."

As he headed towards the door, I found myself suddenly wanting to reach out to grab his arm, but I didn't. Instead, I let him walk away.

Once I was alone, I fell asleep almost instantly.

In my dreams, I created an alternative ending where I had stopped Gabe from leaving. Instead, he laid me on the bed and pulled my clothes off, revealing my curves and dips. He bent low, inhaling my scent with nothing between us.

His fingers slid up my slit, sending tingles through my core and making me shiver. When they found my clit, they moved in a circular motion, teasing me with just the right amount of pressure.

"Gabe," I gasped, arching my back to meet him. "Please." I wanted him inside me more than I had wanted anything before.

He smiled and moved his hands away, leaving me wanting more. Grabbing my wrists, he held them above my head and pushed me deeper into the bed. With one hand firmly keeping me in place, he brought the other to my center. He started slow at first, applying light pressure as he moved his fingers in and out, teasing me until I begged for release. I moaned as he increased the pressure of his movements, pushing me ever closer to completion until I was trembling beneath him.

"You're mine, Ella," Gabe growled. His wolf pushed to the front, teeth bared. "Mine."

He moved his body up over mine, grinding our hips together as he entered me. I gasped at the sensation of being filled, eager to take his thrusts as we moved together. Each movement sent waves of pleasure coursing through my veins, and I could feel myself getting closer and closer to my climax with every passing second.

I was almost there; so, so close. But it never happened. Instead, the dream drifted away, and I was left alone, a shaken mess in the tangled sheets.

The sunlight streaming through the blinds woke me up, but it was the smell coming from the kitchen that had me rolling out of bed. I hadn't slept well after the steamy sex dream, and I was a little nervous to face Gabe after picturing us... together.

But I would have to face him sooner or later, seeing as I was still in his apartment. I gathered all my courage and made my way to the kitchen.

Gabe wasn't lying about being a good cook, that's for sure. He had pulled out all the stops setting up quite a feast on the bar counter - an array of fruits, bacon, eggs, and freshly brewed coffee.

He smiled warmly as he saw me standing in the doorway. "I thought you might be hungry after last night," he said by way of explanation.

I nodded slowly. *He couldn't have seen my dreams, could he?*

My mouth already beginning to water at the sight of all that food. As I sat at the counter, Gabe passed me a plate and started piling it with goodies from every dish. It was like being treated to a five-star meal that, for once, I wasn't in charge of making. I finished everything on my plate and went back for seconds, struggling to avoid making eye contact as I again relived some of the sensations from last night.

"When you said I might be hungry, you couldn't see, you know…my dreams or anything, right?" I tried to play it casual, but I really needed to know how far this mate connection went, especially because I hadn't been privy to his thoughts since he had blocked me out.

My offhanded tone did nothing to fool him.

"Why do you ask, mate?" His lips quirked upward as the heat in his eyes brightened. "Something you didn't want me to see?"

I threw him a look and took a massive bite of syrupy pancake. "Just answer the question, Gabe."

"No, unfortunately. It seems like the situation with the mating mark has impeded some of our connection. I tried to reconnect with you several times already, but it looks like we'll need to wait until we have mated to resume the bond."

Gabe's scowl told me all I needed to know. He was pissed about that.

"Um, sorry, I guess," I said, not sure how else to respond. I immediately cringed after saying it, though. As if this morning could get any more awkward.

"Don't worry, Ella. I'm going to fix this. I have it all planned out."

"You do?" I raised my brows.

He nodded. "Yep. I was going to wait until you finished breakfast to tell you, but now's as good a time as any."

I stiffened, setting my fork down mid-bite. Whatever this was, I could tell it was going to be big. Gabe smiled at my reaction, his teeth flashing in an almost intimidating way. Of course, that was silly. Gabe being intimidating didn't seem possible.

"After you went to bed, I did some thinking about our situation," he said. "I thought about what you need and what I need."

He paused, causing me to frown. "And what is that, exactly?"

"As much as I hate to admit him being right about anything, Neil wasn't wrong when he said that you need someone who offers you dominance in a relationship. I can feel it when I'm with you, and I see it every time I get close to offering you something like that. You melt, and it's the sexist thing in the world if I'm being completely honest."

It was like the air was sucked out of the room. Suddenly, I wasn't interested at all in the pancakes on my plate. Instead, I felt my heart break out into palpitations, and a bead of sweat formed on my brow. If embarrassment was measured on a scale, I was hitting a nine out of ten, easy.

I felt like I should say something to try and deny it, but as soon as I opened my mouth to argue, Gabe was growling.

"Whatever you're going to say, I'm not interested. We've wasted too much time beating around this, and if we are going to be ready to complete our mating bond by the next full moon, we don't have the luxury of playing games forever.

"Instead, we're going to do this my way, which is honestly how I should have handled things from the start.

You need dominance, and I need to give it to you. You think these feelings you have only go one way, Ella, but you're wrong," he said, leaning in and making me meet his eyes. "Being an omega has nothing to do with not being able to be dominant with you. In fact, because I am so in tune with your feelings, I can read you like a book. I can't wait to start taking advantage of that."

I shifted under his gaze but forced myself not to back down so easily.

"What exactly do you have in mind, Gabe?" I asked. "Whips and chains? Keeping me locked up like Neil did until the next full moon?"

A grin slowly spread over his face. "Not quite."

Gabe leaned closer until we were almost touching. The skin on my arms prickled, mysteriously drawn to him. I found myself holding my breath, wanting to close the last bit of distance between us and run away at the same time.

"I'm going to provide you with what you need, and by the time the full moon is here, you'll no longer be a virgin, and you'll be begging me to mark you with my bite."

I blinked. Not what I was expecting.

"And you think that I'll sleep with you because… you're going to boss me around?"

"That's one way of looking at it." He reached up and brushed some of the hair from my eyes. "As much as this color infuriated me, I have to admit it looks beautiful on you. And I'm glad that we got that small disobedience out of the way because starting now, that's not going to fly."

"It didn't exactly fly before," I pointed out. My ass was sore for at least a few days after the visit to the beauty shop.

Gabe gave me a wicked grin. "That was just the start, baby."

Chapter 17

I tried to put my foot down and stay at Mariam's house, but Gabe wouldn't hear it. He wouldn't even let me sleep in his spare room or on the couch. If I wanted to go somewhere, he was right at my heels. It was overwhelming after being on my own for the past how-ever-many years. Thankfully, having dinner with my sister gave me some breathing room.

"How do you stand this?" I complained to Mariam at the alpha house later that evening. I was dressed in an outfit selected by Gabe, smelling of the perfume that he had sitting out for me. It had hints of cinnamon, which made me think of him. That was probably the point, come to think of it.

Mariam just laughed. "Gabe has always been a bit of a stickler for rules, but I think this is a side of him only you bring out," she said with an understanding smile.

I glared at her. "Seriously, is this what it's like between you and Trace? I don't remember Mom having her clothes hand selected by Dad. Or her not being able to go anywhere without him."

"Sure, Trace tries to control just about everything, but it

doesn't always work out how he plans. And we'll never really know the ins and outs of Mom and Dad's relationship. What we saw was probably the tip of the iceberg". Her smile faded. "I bet some of it has to do with Neil, though. I mean, the part about not letting you out of his sight."

My hands felt clammy. "You mean Jeremy hasn't found him?"

"I'm not sure if Jeremy's even looking, to be honest. I know that Neil's been excommunicated from Dark Claw, but I'm not sure if there's an active search or anything. And until your mating bond is set, Gabe probably doesn't want to risk any more issues with him turning up."

I had to sigh. Yeah, that made a lot of sense.

"So that means soon things will let up, right?"

She shrugged again, but something in her expression said it was just as likely to never change.

Gabe kept me close to his side during dinner as if he thought I might try to bolt away into the night. I managed to slink away when my phone vibrated and snuck off into the hallway for some privacy.

I hesitated at the unregistered number before accepting the call.

"Ella." The voice on the other end turned my blood to ice. My wolf whined, unsure of what to do, and I, too, felt a strange combination of conflicting emotions run through me.

"What do you want, Neil?" I hissed. I glanced around the hallway, making sure that no one was there to overhear me.

"Is that any way to greet your mate, baby?" His voice

was like music to my ears, even as his words made me nauseous. "I'm coming for you, Ella. We need to complete our bond, and then no one can keep us apart. You can't tell me that you still don't feel me there in the back of your mind."

It should have been easy enough to lie because I hadn't felt him, at least not since I had arrived at Tumblewild, but now that I was hearing his voice, it was all coming back to me. I fought over wanting to hang up or stay on the line just to hear him speak. Neil's words were like a cold drink of water.

"Goddess, I can't wait to claim you," Neil murmured, clearly as affected as I was. His breathing turned ragged, and I realized what he was doing on the other end of the line. Knowing that he was aroused sent a thrill of desire through me. I squeezed my legs together, refusing to masturbate over the phone to his voice.

Stunned and flushed with embarrassment, I ground out a warning. "Don't call me again."

I quickly hung up the phone, my heart pounding, and my cheeks hot. I leaned against the wall and tried to catch my breath, and it was only then that I realized Gabe was standing in the hallway, watching.

"Ella," he said softly. "Who were you talking to?"

I could feel myself blushing even more as I shook my head and forced a smile. "Just an old friend," I lied, trying to act casual. "Let's go back to dinner."

Gabe didn't move. His eyes were blazing as he glared at me. "Don't lie to me, Ella," he growled. "That wasn't some friend."

I felt my heart drop into my stomach as I realized that he

heard at least part of the conversation. My shoulders slumped as I bowed my head in shame. Gabe was silent for a moment before speaking again.

"Are you going tell me the truth?" He demanded, his voice tight with frustration and anger. "Or do we need to handle this another way?"

His words cut through me like a knife, and I found myself struggling to breathe as feelings of dread and arousal mixed. Gabe's nostrils flared, scenting my desire. He closed the distance between us, backing me into a bathroom and shutting the door behind him.

He grabbed me by the waist and looked into my eyes, his unmoving and passionate gaze. Gabe eased back onto the counter and wasted no time picking me up. He set me down over his lap, ignoring my protests.

His hand came down hard on my backside, using his other arm to brace me against his thighs. With each swat, he growled out a question. "Are you going to tell me who you were talking to?"

I yelped in pain as he continued with unrelenting force until finally, I couldn't take it anymore and screamed out the truth.

"Neil!" Tears of humiliation streamed down my cheeks as I buried my face into my hands in shame. He kept spanking me until all the tension between us melted away, my tears had abated, and my butt felt warm and numb.

Finally, he helped me off his lap and wrapped his arms around me.

"I know," he whispered. "I mean, I knew who it was. I knew as soon as I saw the conflicted look on your face and scented your desire in the air that it was him, and that scares the shit out of me, Ella."

"Join the club," I said under my breath. "You think I wanted him to call me?"

Gabe pulled me up until we were face-to-face. I tried to look away, ashamed of trying to hide the call from him and for letting him take me over his knee again. I wanted to push his hand away and run, but my body betrayed me. The arousal from the spanking, the phone call, hearing Neil's voice. It was too much. I rushed to force my lips against his.

He relented, groaning and allowing himself a taste. I ground against him, using the friction of his pants to help with the ache. I settled my hands on his belt, grappling with the buckle until his length was free. My eyes widened when I wrapped my hand around the length of his dick. It was so big…and warm. It moved for me, hard and silky at the same time. Gabe moaned a curse before pushing me away.

"I'm not going to fuck you while you're thinking of another male," he growled, tucking himself back in.

It took me a second to process his rejection, for the reality of what this meant to settle in. I felt my eyes fill with tears as I sagged against him, too emotionally exhausted to argue or plead. Gabe tried to hold me, but that only made me crave his touch even more.

"Ella," his voice was now soothing, but it was too late. I unlocked the door and fled to the hallway, pulling my skirt down over my abused backside. Mariam rounded the corner, intercepting me as I tried to make an escape.

"Whoa, Ella. Are you okay?"

"No," I replied, my voice shaking. "I just need to leave. I

need some space."

She stepped aside, allowing me to pass without another word. Taking a deep breath, I stumbled outside to the driveway, hesitating only to consider the best course of action. I could shift but leaving as a wolf would make me easier to track if Gabe decided to follow me. It was eerie that he wasn't already. The fact that he had let me go without so much as a grumble reaffirmed that space was what we needed.

That could change at any moment, though.

I took the keys out of my purse and slid into the driver's seat. I pulled away as fast as I could, desperate to put some distance between myself and Gabe.

I had to get away from him. At least, I think that's what I wanted to do.

The night air was cool against my heated skin, but it did little to quell the chaotic emotions churning inside me. My head spun from everything that had happened, and all the tears shed in such a short time frame. As reality began to sink in, all I wanted more than anything was for this day —this mess— to end.

I fiddled with the locking necklace Gabe had placed around my neck earlier that day. After announcing that he would be the dominant one in our relationship, he pulled the necklace out of his pocket, handling it like it was made of glass rather than solid gold.

"It was my grandmother's," he said. "Our family has a tradition. The females wear a necklace as a sign of ownership. Some call it a collar."

The idea made me bristle. "A collar, like as in you own me?"

"Bingo." Gabe's smile had melted away the angry retort I had to that. I had wanted someone more domineering. Maybe ownership wouldn't be that bad.

I shook my head, trying to rid myself of the memory. Maybe now I was getting a mate who was more dominant, even to the point of wanting to own me, but what good was that if he refused to even touch me? Bile rose in my throat at the way he had outright rejected my advances.

The open road leading to Flagstaff was an inviting sight, and I allowed myself to get lost in its familiarity as I drove. I breathed deeply, taking in the cool night air to clear my mind of all negative thoughts.

I wasn't driving with any particular goal in mind, but soon the city buildings replaced the lush countryside that was home to the Tumblewild pack.

I slowed as I approached a familiar building with an old-fashioned wooden sign that read *The Black Bear* in bold letters. It was a bar, one that looked like it had been around for years, given the worn decor. It certainly seemed popular among the locals, with heavy foot traffic coming in and out the doors.

I had never been in a bar, had never even considered it. But at that moment, the temptation to go inside was strong, and the idea of getting lost in a sea of strangers sounded more appealing than returning home alone. But I hesitated— what would happen if I had a drink or two? Would Gabe be upset? Could he be when alcohol wasn't one of the rules he had given to me?

I mentally rattled the new rules off in my head. *No going anywhere with another male alone, dress in the clothes Gabe picks out, try to run plans by him first when possible...*

He had said there would be more added later or as needed. I never even agreed to follow these rules, per se, but I also didn't really put up very much of a fight about it. As weird as it was to admit it, having the rules made me feel a little cared for and maybe even a little turned on.

With that thought in mind, a wave of newfound confidence crashed over me, and I pulled into the parking lot. I grabbed the little beaded clutch that Gabe had given me and stepped out, taking a few deep breaths before walking inside.

The bar was bustling with people laughing, chatting, and dancing. Music filled the air and mixed in with the smell of beer, sweat, and cigarette smoke. I looked around briefly before making my way to an opening at the bar. Even though rowdy conversations filled the room, it was oddly calming for me.

I ordered a vodka cranberry from the bartender, who gave me an understanding smile before quickly sliding my drink across the countertop. Vodka cranberry was the only drink I knew. It was something Mariam would order when she went out with her friends, and I could see why-- it wasn't half bad. I quickly drank that one, enjoying the way it warmed me and caused my brain to quiet.

When I set down the empty glass, the bartender was already making me another. I gratefully accepted it but decided to pace myself. I took a sip of the tart, sugary beverage, and someone caught my eye from across the crowded room – a tall man wearing a black leather jacket with tattoos running up his neck and sleeve. He had been watching me since I sat down at the bar, and when our eyes met, he made his way to me with purposeful strides.

He held out his hand. "Care to dance?" he asked.

My heart raced at his invitation. I had never been asked to dance before, and the idea made me feel alive. I hesitated for a moment before placing my hand in his. His touch was warm and welcoming, but it didn't shoot through me the way it did with Neil.

Gabe, I quickly corrected myself. *It didn't feel like it did with Gabe.*

He pulled me close as we swayed to the music, our movements in perfect harmony with one another. We continued dancing for what seemed like hours until the music finally stopped, and he leaned down to whisper in my ear: "Do you want another drink?"

I was about to answer but felt my wolf snap to attention, stopping my response. There were eyes on me somewhere in the room, but I couldn't tell where they were coming from. The crowd was too big and noisy, and my buzz made my head fuzzy.

I excused myself from the stranger, saying I needed to use the restroom. He nodded and stepped aside, allowing me to leave. I quickly made my way through the crowd and finally stumbled into the hallway where the restrooms were located. Just as I reached for the door handle, a hand grabbed my arm and pushed us both in together. Startled, I turned to see Neil standing there with an intensity in his eyes that took my breath away.

He held onto my arm firmly, not letting go as he spoke with a tight jaw: "Surprised to see me, Ella?" His voice was low and menacing but also filled with an edge of desire.

Without waiting for an answer, he pushed me against the wall, locking the door behind us. His face was only inches away now, his lips dangerously close to mine as he continued speaking in hushed tones: "I know what you want, Ella. I know you've been thinking about me. You want to be with me, don't you?" His words made my body tingle, and I felt a rush wash over me like never before.

At that moment, it was clear – Neil knew exactly how aroused I was because he felt the same way, too. The air between us thickened as he pulled me in closer, our lips inches apart as if daring me to make the first move.

Finally, it was too much to resist. Our lips met with an urgency that felt like it had been building up from weeks of anticipation. It sent shockwaves through my body as if we were trying to consume each other. Neil's hands moved quickly, running his spare hand up my shirt as our tongues explored each other. I felt alive and free as he moved down to my neck and collarbone, his breath hot against my skin. His touch was electric, sending thrills of pleasure through me like nothing ever had before.

I gasped as Neil pushed his hips against mine, grinding his hardness against my core. I felt him grow even thicker as he continued moving, thrusting himself against me.

The only thing keeping us from fucking were a few flimsy pieces of fabric. I grabbed his shoulders, willing him to go harder, harder.

"I knew you wouldn't try to remove my mark," he growled in my ear. "You know this is right. Together we can return to Dark Claw. You'll set Jeremy straight on what happened between us, and we'll start over as the pack's beta couple."

I felt something stir inside of me. My wolf snapped to attention, free from her temporary haze.

I shouted my anger, pushing against him with all my might. His grip loosened, and I was able to break my arm free, launching myself at him and taking him down to the ground. At first, he welcomed my aggression. The fire in his eyes told me he was turned on by it even.

It only took me fumbling with my purse for a split second, and then he was howling, the sensual heat in his gaze replaced with the burn of pepper spray.

I left him on the floor and rushed back to the door, eager to put some distance between the cursing beta and myself. I only made it a few steps when I collided with someone else, another male who soothed my wolf's nerves instantly.

"I'm sorry," I breathed, looking up at Gabe. "I don't know how he found me, but we need to get out of here. It won't take him long to shake off the mace, and when he does, he's going to be out for blood."

Gabe gave me a hard look, his expression blank. He gently nudged me to the side, ignoring my pleas to run. Instead, he let himself into the bathroom and closed the door behind him, sliding the lock back in place.

"Come on, Ella." I felt a tug on my shirt and turned to find my sister. Surprisingly, there was no crowd forming behind her. In fact, there wasn't so much as a concerned employee checking in to see if we were alright. No one in the entire bar seemed to care about Neil getting pummeled and cursing up a storm in the bathroom. "Gabe can handle it. Let's get you out of here."

"But Neil--"

"Jeremy's on his way, and Trace is waiting outside with

backup to take Neil into custody. Gabe just wanted to be the one to kick his ass first," Mariam said, smirking.

I bit my lip and nodded, following her outside. I couldn't help smiling to myself at the sound of Gabe beating the shit out of Neil in the women's restroom.

Chapter 18

"Not. One. Word," Gabe said, gripping the steering wheel a little harder than necessary.

"At least I'm not horny anymore," I said, ignoring the warning and trying to lighten the mood. "This would be a lot worse if I was still horny."

"Because you were before? What, in the bathroom?" I opened my mouth to answer, but he shut me down with another glare. "I still can't believe you were throwing back drinks in a bar."

I slumped back into my seat and looked out the window. It was well past midnight at this point. The alcohol had long since worn off, thankfully, but now I was left with a small headache and an empty stomach. At least Neil wouldn't be a problem anymore.

"Can we please stop for some food?" I threw in a pitiful frown, hoping it would win me some points. It must have worked because Gabe pulled into the next drive-thru, grumbling as he did so.

Moments later, I had a huge burrito and soda, eternally grateful for the instant availability of fast food.

"So, you aren't talking to me, right?" I asked,

unwrapping the burrito carefully.

Gabe refused to smile. "If I am, it's not working so well. Do you have any idea what Neil was planning to do to you? What would have happened if I hadn't been able to track your scent in the parking lot?"

"And what if you hadn't guessed the right bar?" I chimed in, mouth full. "Yeah, I know what he wanted. I was the one who maced him."

"Not helping," he said, scowling. "I'm serious, Ella."

I swallowed the bite of burrito, feeling the weight of his words.

"I'm sorry, okay? I didn't mean to put myself in danger. I just... I didn't know how to handle it."

He nodded sharply. "I understand. You didn't know how to handle your attraction to him."

Whoa. What? I set the burrito down. "No. I didn't know how to handle being rejected by you while I had your penis in my hands."

Gabe swerved and slammed on the brakes, bringing the car to an abrupt stop on the side of the road. I braced myself against the dashboard, my heart racing.

"What did you just say?" he asked, his voice low and dangerous.

I swallowed hard, realizing too late that my filter had failed me. "I'm sorry," I said quickly. "I didn't mean to say that out loud."

"You didn't answer my question," he said, his eyes locked on mine. "Rejection while holding... what did you mean by that?"

I took a deep breath, knowing I couldn't lie my way out of this. "I meant that I was attracted to you and throwing myself at you, and then you rejected me."

There it was. The truth, out there in the open between us. I waited for Gabe to say something - anything - but he just stared at me. My heart raced as the moments passed, and I began worrying that this might have been a mistake. I shouldn't have been so vulnerable, so open with my raw feelings.

Gabe's expression was unreadable. Then he reached out and cupped my cheek, his thumb brushing against my skin. His touch sent a shock of electricity down my spine, and I could feel my entire body responding to it.

"Ella," he said softly. "I think you know I have feelings for you, too." He leaned in closer, his lips barely an inch away from mine. He reached between us and touched the locking necklace. "I've wanted you ever since the day I met you. Before I saw you, even. You have to know how hard it's been to keep my hands off you. To keep myself from acting on… everything until you were ready."

I scoffed. "Really? Until I was ready? Dry humping you in the bathroom didn't indicate I was 'ready' enough?"

This time, Gabe didn't even try to hide his grin. "It was a start, mate. But you had to be ready. For everything, not just sex."

"I need specifics. Ready for what, exactly?"

"For everything you've been fighting me on. Our bond. Being mine, permanently." Gabe eased back onto the road. "Don't get me wrong. I love that you're looking forward to the sex. I am, too. But I need you to be ready to welcome my bite. And I've only got a few days to get you there."

"I think I'm closer to that than you think," I whispered. It felt weird to admit it to myself, let alone say it aloud.

"But maybe, if we have sex first, it will bring us closer, and then it will be easier to accept the mark."

Gabe didn't answer right away. His eyes remained focused on the road, and I could feel the tension inside of him rev up. My eyes fell to his lips when he licked them. His jaw ticked where he was gritting his teeth.

We pulled into Gabe's apartment complex around two in the morning. I was tired and ready for bed but grateful to not be tied up in the trunk of Neil's car. Or worse, to be throwing myself into his arms.

I instantly chilled at the thought. I didn't want to be with Neil, but did that mean I would be sleeping alone again tonight? Or was Gabe's resolve starting to soften?

I'd get my answer soon enough.

Gabe grabbed my hand and tugged me up the stairs to his front door. He let us in, the familiar living room greeting us with its warm colors and comfortable furniture. Gabe led me down the short hallway to his bedroom.

A soft light shone through the blinds, filtering onto the bed where his two pillows were propped up against the headboard. He gestured for me to sit on the edge of the bed, and I complied without hesitation.

My eyes widened as his hands went to his belt. He unbuckled his pants, letting his tented boxers spill out.

"You're a vixen, Ella. I've tried to wait, but there's only so much teasing you can expect me to take before I have a release. If you think you're ready for my cock, I need you to show me just how eager you are."

His words sent a thrill through me. I wanted this. I wanted him, but now that he was offering himself to me, I hesitated.

"I don't know what to do," I admitted, barely speaking above a whisper. My face burned. Of course, I knew the basic mechanics of everything, but I didn't know exactly what he wanted from me.

Gabe chuckled and cupped my face in his hands. "It's okay, Ella. I'll show you." He leaned forward, kissed me deeply, and then traced his lips down my neck. His mouth lingered at the base of my throat, making my breathing hitch and my skin flush with pleasure.

He gently moved my hands to the front of his pants, helping me push the fabric down so that his rigid manhood was completely exposed. The head was red and bulbous like it was angry to be so hard. A few beads of wetness slipped out of the slit on the head of his cock. I ran my fingers lightly over the veiny ridges that wrapped around him. He groaned and swore at my touch, causing me to smile.

He positioned my lips near the head before running his thumb along the length. "Start by licking it," he said, his voice low and gravelly with desire. I obeyed, tasting the wetness on his skin. A shudder ran through him in response to my touch.

He guided my movements with gentle nudges as I explored every inch of him with my tongue. Every stroke was rewarded with soft moans as he began to thrust into my mouth.

I kept up with him, adapting to his pace with each thrust. His grip on the back of my head became more urgent, his hands tangled in my hair. My throat burned, and my eyes blurred. For a terrifying moment, I couldn't breathe. Without warning, Gabe threw his head back and let out an ecstatic moan as jets of warm cum filled up my throat.

I panicked as the salty liquid spilled from the sides of my mouth. Gabe continued thrusting, slower now, as though he was trying to push more of it down into my tummy.

"That's my good girl. Take all my cum, mate," he whispered.

He softened and slowed, pulling himself from me. Gabe touched the sides of my mouth where some of the cum had escaped. He carefully rubbed it into my skin, making circles on my cheeks and neck, until it was gone.

"Don't waste my cum, Ella. It either stays on you or inside you, but it's not going to waste."

I woke up in the late morning, my body still tangled with Gabe's. I had rolled over in my sleep and was now facing him. His face was illuminated by the sun streaming through the window, his eyes shut but a peaceful smile on his lips. He looked beautiful. I watched him for a moment, taking in his features.

I shifted and felt his erection hard pressed up against my thigh. A satisfied sigh escaped my lips as I realized he wanted me in his sleep. The motion was enough to make him stir awake. His gaze was full of lust, sending a thrill through my body. As much as I loved sucking him, we had ended things short of actually having sex, and the anticipation was driving me crazy, just like he planned.

Gently, he brushed his thumb across my bottom lip before leaning in for a kiss. It was slow and passionate at first but then grew wilder as our desire for each other built between us. He deepened the kiss as his hands roamed down to cup my breasts through the thin fabric of my shirt, making me moan with pleasure beneath him.

He rolled on top of me, taking control. His hands squeezed my butt as he rocked his hard cock back and forth, sending a delicious jolt of pleasure through my body. It was so erotic, so hot. I could feel the wetness between my legs and the ache in my core, begging him to be inside me.

I wanted to rip my clothes off and feel his skin against mine, but I couldn't quite make myself move. "Is there any particular reason you're not taking this off?" he asked, his voice deep and hoarse with arousal.

I finally managed to get my hands moving, slipping them under the hem of my shirt to find skin. I must not have been moving quickly enough for him because Gabe pushed my hands away with a dissatisfied growl.

Without warning, he gripped the top with two hands and tore the shirt in two, taking my bra with it.

I froze, completely exposed to him for the first time in the privacy of his bedroom. As humiliating as it was to be naked in front of him in the woods, this felt a million times more intimate. But for the first time, I soaked up the look of approval in his eyes. In a moment of pure need, I grabbed the back of his head and brought him down to my chest, needing to feel his lips on my nipples.

He grinned against my skin before wrapping his lips around one of my tiny pink buds and sucking. I arched my back, pressing myself into his mouth as he licked and sucked my sensitive skin. I could feel the pressure building up inside me as he toyed with my body. My entire core was focused on the sensation of his tongue and mouth on my nipple, making me squirm beneath him.

Gabe left me with a kiss on my breast before moving to the next one, giving it the same attention. My eyes fluttered shut as I relished the sensations flooding my body. The pressure in my core had reached a near-unbearable level. Gabe's skilled mouth on my breasts had me ready to make the most embarrassing noises. I had to touch him. I had to feel him.

I reached down and found his shaft again. It was hot and hard as steel under my fingertips. Thick. Exactly how I remembered.

I gave the tip a tentative stroke, and Gabe moaned against my breast. "I can't get enough of you," he growled against my chest.

I wasn't sure how much more of his mouth I could take, but I didn't want to break the spell. I pulled my knees up to give him room to kneel between my legs. I was anxious to feel him slide into me.

His rippling muscles were hard under my fingers. I traced a line down his chest and over his abs until I reached his hardness. He shifted and pulled me to my feet. The heat in his eyes made me catch my breath.

I had to feel him inside of me. I hadn't realized that I was practically panting with anticipation. He moved to stand in front of me, his cock jutting from his hips. I leaned in to kiss it, but Gabe jerked back, not letting me taste him. His eyes were full of fire as he bent down and kissed my neck, trailing his hot mouth down to my breasts. He grabbed the waistband of my pants with both hands and in one motion, he yanked them down my legs.

My only thought was relief. The ache was too much for my underwear. I wanted to feel him against me. In me. Anywhere.

"Mmm," I moaned, my eyes tracing the ridges of his abs, down past his cock, and further still to the delicious V of his hips. He was so much more than I remembered.

He smiled at me, his eyes dark with lust. He leaned down and kissed me again, his hand stroking my clit. It slid down between my legs and inside me, filling me. "You're so wet for me," he mumbled against my lips, his breath hot against my mouth. He slid in a second finger, and I moaned, my body arching to meet his hand. My hips rocked against him, and I got greedy, wanting even more. He obliged and slipped in a third, pumping his fingers inside me.

I broke the kiss and buried my face against his bare shoulder, crying out as he pushed his fingers deeper and harder inside me.

"You're so wet," he panted again in my ear, "so wet for me. I could fuck you all day. I could fuck you 'til you couldn't walk. I would take you apart and put you back together again."

I felt his hand slide away from my core, and he gripped my hair, pulling my head back and staring into my eyes. I could smell myself on his fingers. "I want you," he said, his voice full of passion. "Tell me you want this."

"I want it," I whispered. I had to have him. There was no way I could hold back after that. I needed to feel him inside me.

He grabbed my arm and pulled me to the edge of the bed, bending me over. The vulnerability of him seeing everything turned me on like nothing else. I was completely at his mercy. I wanted to belong to him.

Gabe leaned over and pulled my hair back, exposing my neck. My heart skipped a beat when I remembered Neil's mark was still displayed there. His teeth grazed my skin, sending a shiver through my body. It was a promise. That mark wouldn't be there for long.

I felt the head of his cock nudge my folds apart, and I braced myself for the first thrust.

"Relax," he hissed. I felt him press against my tightness, slowing so he wouldn't hurt me.

I did my best to unclench so that Gabe could enter me. He gripped his cock and lined it up with my hole, pressing into me until I was completely filled with him. I cried out at the intrusion. My body stretched to accommodate him, and the feeling was raw and overwhelming.

"Tell me, mate. Tell me how full I make you."

"It's too much, Gabe," I breathed, groaning. I wasn't lying. At first, it was too much, but I was also incredibly wet, coating him enough so that soon he was pumping in and out of me easily.

"You can take it. You were meant to take it," he growled above me. Gabe reached down between us and began playing with my clit, sending tremors through me. I jerked against his pounding rhythm, each time unsure if I could take the full length again.

It didn't seem to matter. My body was his, and he continued to thrust into me harder and harder. His teeth sank into my shoulder. It wasn't a mating bite, but it was a way to prevent himself from biting my neck.

As he thumped into me, I could feel him swell again.

From the night before, I knew that the swelling meant he was getting close to shooting himself inside me. Then, I felt a different pressure start to build until it was too much to take, and I screamed. Outright, actual screams.

Gabe groaned and shoved himself into me one final time, releasing his warm seed inside my body. He collapsed on top of me, and we lay there in a sweaty heap, our heartbeats racing together. I could feel him harden again inside me, and I let out a groan.

"Are you okay?" he asked, suddenly concerned.

"Mhmm." I was so content I was almost purring. I trailed a finger down his chest. "That was… intense."

"I told you. I've wanted you for too long to hold back now that I have you."

I smiled at him, swallowing hard. "I don't know what this all means, Gabe. I just know that I want you. I want you, too."

"Good. Because I don't plan on letting you go." He moved, and his hardness felt rough against my raw passage. Gabe started sawing in and out again, using his semen as lubrication.

I moaned and panted. "Fuck, that feels so good."

I grinned and had to blush at my own language. The old Ella would have never used words like that. Gabe must have realized the same thing.

"You don't know what it does to me when you say something dirty, mate. Tell me exactly how good it feels."

So, I did.

Chapter 19

It felt like my body was being torn in two directions.

Not just from all the sex, although after a few very active days with Gabe, I was feeling that, as well. No, the issue I had was something deeper. It was on a spiritual and emotional level.

I was wearing the mark of one werewolf and sleeping with another. The old Ella would have been completely scandalized by that, but at the moment, I was just thankful one of those werewolves was also my true mate, and there wasn't a third male in the mix.

My standards of decency had hit an all-time low, that's for sure. Gabe was adamant that this was a temporary situation. Soon, I would have his mark instead and feel so much less conflicted.

Goddess, I hoped so. My wolf wouldn't last if this went on indefinitely. She was thoroughly pleased with me for finally sleeping with our mate, but now the other male's mark irritated her even more than it had before. She was tense, ready to attack Neil at any moment. As much as I shared her sentiments, I also hoped never to see him again.

Unfortunately, even that wasn't a guarantee. After all, I

never found out what happened to Neil after I left the bar. Was he in Dark Claw? Was he even still alive? I considered not asking about it, but the uncertainty of not knowing was getting to be too much.

I glanced at Gabe as he drove. "Do you know where Neil is?" I asked, trying and failing terribly to sound casual.

The look of bliss on his face slipped, and he shifted uncomfortably in his seat.

"Why do you ask?"

I rolled my eyes. "Because after countless hours in bed with you, I plan on running off to find the maniac who tried to rape me."

Gabe scowled. "Watch the tone, Ella."

"Fine," I said. "I just want to know that he's gone for good."

I watched Gabe's tension melt away, like there was any question I was committed to him. It hurt a little to see him seriously doubt me like that. "Do you really think I would still want him?" I asked.

"I know that the rational part of you never did, but until you're wearing my mark on your neck, my wolf isn't going to be satisfied."

"Well, mine isn't, either," I grumbled. I hadn't intended to say that out loud, but when Gabe's face lit up, and he reached for my hand, I was happy that I did.

We spent the rest of the drive like that, holding hands, his thumb making small circles on my palm. For the first time in a long time, I was able to just relax and enjoy the moment. Tomorrow was the full moon. We planned to go to the pack run and end the evening with me accepting Gabe's mating bite. Since we had definitely consummated the relationship in every other way— multiple times, in fact— the mating bite should be enough to bind us together.

As for right now, I wasn't entirely sure where we were going. I thought maybe he wanted to do something romantic and try to inspire that side of our relationship, which also felt brand new. But that wasn't his plan at all, and nothing would have prepared me for the dread of pulling into a parking space in front of the downtown diner.

I groaned and slumped in my seat. "Why are we here?" I asked, already guessing the answer.

Gabe smiled sadly, feeling my discomfort. "Samantha's working today," he said. "She wanted to see you and asked if we would stop by."

My heart sank into my stomach as I looked at the diner's windows and saw Samantha inside, smiling and easily taking orders from customers. She had a lot more confidence than me when it came to dealing with people, and I just didn't feel like facing her again after she had lied about their relationship.

"Ella, please?" Gabe asked with desperation in his voice. He must have sensed that I was on the edge of saying no. "Trust me. Sometimes people just need another chance to make things right."

I know he isn't talking about me specifically, but my mind instantly goes back to the times I hurt him. Gabe had always given me another chance. Of course, he would do the same for anyone he cared about.

"Fine," I said. "But you're buying me a milkshake."

Even though Gabe insisted that he makes all the

decisions for us, I still liked knowing that he wouldn't have made me go inside if I really didn't want to. He pushed me just enough without actually becoming an asshole.

The bell chimed over the door as he opened it for us, and Samantha turned around, her eyes going wide when she saw me. She quickly composed herself and smiled weakly, walking around the counter.

"Ella, I'm so glad you came. I'm about to go on break, so go ahead and have a seat. I'll be right back."

She kept her eyes on me the entire time, not even glancing in Gabe's direction. It was subtle, but it went a long way to making my wolf feel better.

Still, she wasn't a fan. *The female who wants our mate doesn't deserve our time*, she said.

I couldn't disagree with that, but I'd stay for a little while for Gabe's sake.

We sat down, and a few minutes later, Samantha joined us with two milkshakes in her hands. She gave one to each of us before sitting across from me. She messed with the front of her apron, fidgeting and betraying her nervousness.

"I'm so sorry for what I did," she blurted out. "I know you must hate me, Ella, and I don't blame you. I was wrong to lie about my relationship with Gabe. He's never been more than a friend, even when I wanted more." She looked at Gabe briefly before returning her gaze to me. "You don't deserve to be lied to or taken advantage of, and I won't do that ever again."

Under the table, Gabe reached out and grabbed my hand, squeezing it gently. I kept my eyes on Samantha, considering how to respond.

"I can understand why you did it," I said carefully. "Honestly, I thought something was going on between the two of you anyway. Otherwise, I probably would have brushed it off when Gabe said it wasn't true. But no matter what, I should have trusted him, and that was my mistake."

Samantha visibly relaxed. Her eyes darted between Gabe and me as though she was seeing us together for the first time. Her eyes were tired and more than a little sad.

"I hope you'll consider me a friend," she said. "Both of you."

I wasn't sure about all that, but it was a kind gesture, and I could tell she meant it sincerely. At least now, moving to Tumblewild would be a little less awkward. Trying to avoid another member with a pack this size wasn't exactly easy. More importantly, I knew her saying that meant a lot to Gabe.

"Thanks, Samantha. We should be going, but we'll see you at the pack run tonight, right?"

She nodded and refused to take Gabe's money for the milkshakes. I smiled to myself when he left the money as a tip anyway. He was a good guy, and that wasn't the negative thing I used to think it was.

"So that wasn't the worst thing ever, right?"

My smile turned to a scowl, but I had to admit it wasn't as bad as I thought it would be.

The first ones to run were always the alphas. Sometimes the pack runs started with a speech or special event, and other times the alphas just took off into the woods, trusting that the rest of the pack would follow. Mariam begged me to use this run for our mating ceremony, but we didn't want that.

Or, rather, it wasn't what I wanted.

The idea of having a ceremony with the whole pack present was my own personal nightmare. Since Gabe and I weren't the beta or alpha couple, hosting such a huge celebration was unnecessary. Instead, I imagined our day as something intimate with just a few of our friends and my sister there. Plus, Jeremy wasn't around to help officiate me joining the Tumblewild pack. While it wasn't absolutely necessary that he be present— video calling was an acceptable alternative— that tradition was important to me, too.

That didn't mean we were going to put off the mating bite, of course. Gabe's eyes continued to linger on the tender area right above my collarbone, making my pulse race and my sex throb. The restraint it took to avoid biting me, especially during sex, was taking a toll on him.

I could feel Neil's mark even more during those times, and it was annoying, like a scratch I couldn't itch right. Whenever I touched it, Gabe's gaze would darken even more.

Not for long. I stood next to Gabe now, waiting for Mariam and Trace to lead us into the woods. They had already shifted and were circling each other playfully. Then, without warning, Mariam bolted into the trees, and Trace let out a howl before chasing after her.

The rest of the pack bayed in return as members began shifting and racing to join them. My wolf shook out her fur, stretching to feel the earth under her paws. Gabe caught her eye, and she gave a hearty howl of her own. I thought she would make Gabe chase her, but Gabe's wolf turned and left her in the dust before she could take off.

Two could play that game. My wolf refused to follow his trail and set out in a different direction. She had a streak of mischief in her that loved giving Gabe's wolf a run for his money, and I was more than a little amused to find out how long it would take him to realize she wasn't following him.

Until then, I was relishing in the call of the outdoors with the rest of the pack.

There was something magical about the smell of the forest - mossy and peaceful - that called to me. The light of the full moon illuminated my way, and I savored every moment, feeling my wolf's fur ripple with excitement as she leaped through branches and vines. Every now and then, there would be a loud howl from one of the wolves as they played and reminded each other of the inherent hierarchy within the pack.

Suddenly, the wind shifted directions, and I caught a whiff of Gabe's scent. He was getting closer! Instinctively, my wolf picked up her pace, pushing her body faster than before. What had begun as a silly prank turned into a fight of wills. Would he be able to catch her?

The answer came in the form of a loud growl that vibrated through my chest. Gabe's wolf had finally caught up to her, and he wasn't happy. Instead of yielding to him, my wolf just kept running, too proud to stop now. Gabe's wolf let out another throaty sound, and suddenly it seemed like the forest around us had stilled.

If there were other wolves nearby, I was no longer aware of them. The only thing that mattered was the connection between Gabe and me, and the way our wolves were drawn together.

Before I could process what was happening, Gabe's wolf tackled mine to the ground. He straddled her body and sunk his teeth into her neck without warning. My wolf howled in delight as she felt his teeth dig into her. She threw control back to me, allowing my human form to return. Gabe's wolf relinquished control to him at the same time.

The bite stung, and I could feel blood running from the puncture wounds, but the desire coursing through my veins was much more overwhelming. Wrapping my arms around his neck, we kissed, exploring each other's mouths with a hunger that had been slowly building all day.

Gabe moved one of his hands to cup my breast while the other trailed lower, pushing gently against me until he found what he was looking for. His fingers stroked and teased my sensitive flesh until I was breathless with need.

Gabe must have felt it, too, because he pulled away from our kiss to look into my eyes.

"You're mine, mate."

Slowly, he thrust into me as I gasped at the pleasure of having him inside of me again, feeling every inch of him as he held me in place, forcing me to take all of him again and again.

He moved faster, harder, deeper until I couldn't think straight. His deep, baritone voice was the only thing I could hear. He was promising never to leave me, never to let me down.

My wolf was right.
I was Gabe's mate. I was his.
And that meant he was mine, too.

Chapter 20

I handed Gabe the packing tape, taking a moment to look around the sparse living room. It felt so wrong to see it without any furniture. My parents had lived in the house forever. It had always been home. Now I was preparing for a new home and future in a completely different pack. I finally have what I always wanted: a mate and a future with him. So why did it feel so wrong to leave?

"You okay?" Gabe asked, straightening to stand beside me. The mating bond gave him access to my feelings, but he probably didn't even need it to know I was depressed about the move. I'm sure I had bad vibes radiating off me.

I nodded, taking a deep breath. "Yeah, I'm okay."

Gabe put his arm around me and squeezed. "Spend some time with Heather in the bakery before we go," he suggested. That seemed like a great idea, one last day of normalcy before everything changed forever.

So that's what I did. I spent my last day at the bakery with Heather, baking bread and pastry treats for the morning crowd. We laughed and joked as if nothing had changed, but it felt more like a goodbye than anything else. The hours flew by in a blur until it was time to close up shop.

Heather hugged me tightly. I was getting better with the whole hugging thing, and it felt right to give one to her. "I'm going to miss you so much," she said softly.

"I'm going to miss you too," I said. I gave her a small squeeze before stepping away. "You have to come and visit me, and I'll come back to see how things are going with you, too. Promise?"

Heather nodded, but I knew it would be a long time before we would visit again if it ever happened. Gabe was needed at Tumblewild, and after what happened with Neil escaping custody, he wasn't open to me traveling so far on my own.

We said our last goodbyes before I quickly made my way to my car. Gabe was loading up the last few boxes when I pulled up at the house. He hitched my car to the back of the truck so we could ride together in the U-Haul cab. I packed the bag of snacks and water up front, and we began our drive to Tumblewild.

I stared out the window as we drove away from my old home, a mixture of emotions running through me. An unfamiliar feeling of homesickness had already crept in. I forced it down, determined to focus on the positives of moving.

I'd be with Gabe, of course, but I'd also be able to spend a lot of time with Mariam. Maybe we'd have a chance to actually have a closer relationship.

The thought of being closer to her made me smile, knowing it would mean the world to our parents. I drifted off to sleep, Gabe's hand in mine, listening to the hum of the wheels on the highway.

Two weeks later, I was moved and settled into Gabe's apartment. We were able to mesh our furniture and decor, donating what we didn't need to other pack members. My house in Dark Claw had some new tenants, too. They were a young family, thankful to find a house available on pack lands so they could move out of their apartment. Giving the place up was hard, but it was the right thing to do.

Even though Mariam only lived down the road, we weren't seeing much of each other. As the alpha female, she had a lot of responsibilities and often worked around the clock. Gabe had a lot of work to catch up on, too, after taking off all that time to be with me. Trace had hinted more than once that Gabe would soon be offered an official place on the pack council, which was exciting, even if it meant his workload would increase again. Gabe wanted to really help the pack and make a difference. Being on the council would allow him to do that.

I was excited for him but felt a massive loss after leaving the bakery in Dark Claw. I had no job living in Tumblewild, and it felt like I never really fit in with the other pack members like Mariam did. She meshed with them so well it was almost like she had been in Tumblewild her whole life, and I couldn't help feeling jealous of her once again.

'What's wrong?" Gabe asked that night. He was rubbing my shoulders before bed, which usually made me melt into a puddle of goo, but I couldn't seem to relax at the moment.

"I don't fit in here, Gabe," I complained. "I'm trying, but

there's nothing for me to do here. I don't have the bakery or any friends, really. Mariam is busy, and so are you. I pretty much just hang around the apartment all day."

While staying home and reading all day had been fun at first, I was restless. Gabe gave me a sympathetic look.

"I know change can be tough, Ella, but it will get better. You'll see. We just need to find something here for you to connect with. Maybe you'd like to work down at the cafe. Samantha told me they're hiring."

I made a face, and my wolf growled her disapproval. *Seriously?*

"Okay, bad idea," he said, laughing. "Maybe it would help to go back to Dark Claw and check up on the bakery and the house. You could see that everything's fine and maybe get some ideas about ways you can help out Tumblewild."

"Really? You'd be fine with that?"

Gabe winced. "I don't like the idea of you being alone, what with Neil being free somewhere out there. But I've been working a lot of overtime, and I think I could manage a three-day weekend."

"Are you serious?" Relief washed over me. I'd tried not to let it show, but I had been worried about the bakery. Whenever I texted her, Heather said everything was alright, but the messages were missing any humor or teasing, a dead giveaway that something was wrong.

"Of course. Gotta keep my mate happy," Gabe said, his eyes roaming my body with interest. "Especially when she takes such good care of me."

———

It was worse than I thought it would be. I mean, I'm not exactly sure what I was expecting, but it wasn't that the bakery would be in total chaos and the pack falling apart. Nevertheless, that's what Gabe and I walked into on our first day back.

We checked into the hotel without any indication of things being amiss, but once we started driving to the bakery, it was clear that things were not as they should be. Litter lined the streets on both sides, and kids who should be in school on a Friday morning were running wild in overgrown yards. Closer to downtown, Gabe had to pull over and break up a fight between two pack members, brothers, who were interested in the same female.

Typically, these types of pack issues would be handled by the council, led by the pack beta. Then it hit me: there was no pack beta anymore.

Neil wasn't the best candidate for the job, but he had provided the pack with some structure, at least. The alpha position was intended to be shared between a couple, but Jeremy had to shoulder all those responsibilities without a mate, and now, he was also taking on the work of a beta, most likely.

When we finally arrived at the bakery, it was in a state of chaos. Heather was there alone, trying to manage a full rush of orders with no staff or supplies. She had been waiting for deliveries since early last week, but they hadn't come yet. There were groans from customers as Heather apologized and explained that things were taking longer than usual due to the lack of supplies.

Gabe moved around the kitchen quickly, helping her with whatever she needed. He cracked jokes with the customers while trying to grab orders from them. He wasn't exactly sure what he was doing, but like a true omega, he set everyone at ease. I was back in my element, making espresso with what little stock there was.

"Are either of you looking for a job?" Heather joked when the crowd finally thinned. The mess around us made my head spin.

"I don't understand what happened to the pack," I said. "We've been gone for just a few weeks, and it's anarchy out there."

"And in here," Gabe added. He grimaced at the sticky mess of cups and stir sticks a group of teenagers had left on the bar. I knew his inner neat freak must be horrified.

"Yeah, well, you know the suppliers all go through the council for payment so we can get bulk discounts, but the council never approved the orders, so now there's a food shortage in all the restaurants and the grocery store. Most of the pack has to drive into town, which affects pack funds, of course. Although, who knows what those are like right now, anyway."

"What do you mean?" I asked, sweeping up some crumpled napkins.

"It pissed off about half of the council when Jeremy arrested Neil. People liked him, you know? He can put on a good front. The other council members sided with Jeremy, creating a huge division in the pack. Then, when Neil escaped, everyone who sided with him left, too, and now there's way too much work for the council members remaining to handle it on their own."

I nodded. Things like this had happened to other packs when a key member was corrupt. Sometimes the pack would survive a split, but other times shifters would need to be absorbed by neighboring packs. Dark Claw had been around for generations, but it would probably disappear if something didn't change.

"What can we do to help?" Gabe asked.

"I don't really know. Maybe Jeremy could tell you," Heather said, shrugging sadly.

We helped her clean up the rest of the bakery and hang the closed sign on the door. The bakery would be closed at least until the supply issue was resolved and she could get more help. That much was clear. My heart sank at the thought that the business we had built might never reopen.

"We can't let everything fall apart," I said when Gabe and I returned to the car.

"Let's go see what Jeremy says," he suggested. "Maybe he's already getting things under control. We don't want to jump to any conclusions."

I sighed. Sometimes I wished Gabe wasn't so logical. I wanted to roll up my sleeves and call on Tumblewild for help right away. My wolf agreed. She was as saddened as I was to see how far downhill our pack had gone.

I braced myself as we pulled up to the alpha house. The last time I was there, Neil had tried to force me into a mating bond, so it wasn't someplace I was looking forward to returning.

Surprisingly, it didn't feel as bad as I thought it would. Of course, that was probably because Gabe was there, squeezing my hand reassuringly.

"You okay?" he whispered. I felt a surge of protective love burst through our connection. In our shared consciousness, his wolf nuzzled mine, curling his body reassuringly around her.

"Yep," I said truthfully. I brushed a kiss across his lips and led the way to the front door. Being here again on my own terms and knowing that Neil wouldn't be able to touch me, actually felt really empowering.

Gabe knocked on the door, and we waited. Nothing. He rang the doorbell and knocked again. I was about to call Jeremy and see if we could schedule a meeting when we heard some sounds coming from inside.

Jeremy cracked the door open, squinting at us from the darkness within the house.

"Ella? What are you doing here?"

His eyes were bloodshot, and his speech was slightly slurred.

"We, uh... wanted to talk to you about helping out the pack," Gabe said slowly, his hand still gripping mine.

Jeremy sighed and stepped back, opening the door wider. "Come in."

We followed him into the living room, where he motioned for us to sit down. The slight unsteadiness in his gait told us he was either a little drunk or had just woken up. Maybe both.

"Do you want a drink?" he asked gruffly. We both shook our heads, watching Jeremy make one for himself at the wet bar. "Whatever help you want to offer the pack, it won't be enough to save it. Dark Claw is in shambles, and I'm working on relocating the members who are left."

Gabe and I exchanged a glance. No wonder Jeremy was a wreck.

"Are you sure there are no other options?" I asked. "Have you thought of applying for financial assistance? I bet you would qualify for help with APU."

While every pack was run independently, there were organizations set up to prevent pack failure during times of hardship. The largest, American Packs United, would be able to give Dark Claw a loan or grant to tide them over.

"The council is overwhelmed," Jeremy said. "Even if I had the money, we don't have adequate leadership to keep things going."

Gabe nodded. "What do you need? A new beta and a few council members? Would some of the pack be able to step in temporarily?"

Jeremy sighed and swirled his liquor around in the glass. "A year ago, probably. But pack loyalty is at an all-time low. Even the members who didn't leave with Neil don't really want to step into a leadership role. A lot of them have families and want stability for their kids. Pouring themselves into a failing pack is just too risky."

It was clear that Jeremy was exhausted, both physically and emotionally. He had been trying to hold the pack together for too long and had finally reached his breaking point. I could sense the desperation in him, and I knew my mate could, too.

Gabe leaned forward in his chair. "What if Tumblewild offered to help? We could find other wolves willing to step up and lead the pack temporarily until you can figure out a more permanent solution."

Jeremy looked at us skeptically. "Do you really think it's possible? Dark Claw needs experienced members with proven track records."

Gabe smiled reassuringly. "We know people who would be willing to lend their expertise to the pack, even on a temporary basis. And if that doesn't work, the APU does offer some non-financial assistance. They might be able to send some leadership our way, too."

Jeremy and I stared at Gabe. *Send some leadership our way?* I asked through our mental connection. *Are you including us in this scenario?*

We need to stay and help out here, Gabe answered. *They need us, Ella.*

I nodded, a smile growing on my face. I didn't have a place in Tumblewild, but we were needed here. I could help get the bakery, and the shipments going, and Gabe had lots of experience supporting a thriving pack council. Still, none of that prepared me for what he said next.

"If you'll have me, Jeremy, I'll be your beta," Gabe offered. His voice was strong, unwavering.

Jeremey's eyebrows shot up, clearly as shocked as I was.

"I know I'm an omega by birth, but I have the skills and knowledge to step in as beta. I'm sure you're aware of other instances."

He was right. Sometimes a beta wolf would yield the position to another pack member for the good of the group. In a situation like this, where there really wasn't any other option, a flexible omega could be the pack's only hope.

"Are you prepared to be part of a beta couple, Ella?" Jeremy asked. I could see the gears in his head turning, adjusting to the idea.

It was a good question. Was I prepared for that kind of responsibility? I mean, if Neil and I had worked out, I would have been Dark Claw's beta female anyway. I let out a deep breath and smiled. "Yeah. Yeah, I think I am."

Epilogue

Jeremy let out a weary breath as he settled into his seat. The stately desk wasn't his taste, but it had been in the alpha's office for generations, and he didn't think replacing it was really an option at this point. Keeping it had an odd effect on the room, though. It made it feel so impersonal and intimidating, but that was how the position of alpha of Dark Claw felt to him, anyway. Even several years after stepping into his father's role, most days, Jeremy had a hard time believing that he was really the leader of the pack.

He hadn't always felt like an adequate leader, that's for sure. Especially lately. Neil shouldn't have been in a position of power in the first place. Jeremy could see that now, clear as day. He kicked himself thinking about how he had defended the beta to everyone, never once suspecting he wasn't fit for leadership. Worse even, Jeremy had endangered a pack member by recommending Neil as a chosen mate. Thankfully, Ella seemed to forgive him for that blunder, at least.

He reached under the desk and pulled out a large bottle

of scotch. It was almost empty, a testament to how much stress he had been under the past few weeks. Jeremy told himself he would cut back at some point, but now he relied upon the comfort it brought him. Alcohol helped to numb all the guilt and anxiety. With Neil gone, it was slowly turning into his best friend.

Jeremy frowned as he poured it into the lowball glass. Either the liquor bottles were getting smaller, or he was drinking more. In any case, he would need to stock up again soon. He downed the brown liquid straight, ignoring the burn and waiting for its calming effect to settle in. Impatient for relief, he poured a second glass and then a third.

Slowly, the bad feelings dissipated, and he was able to breathe again.

There was a quiet knock at the door. Jeremy groaned, knowing it would either be his assistant, Grace, or his new beta, Gabriel. Neither option was ideal, especially while he was slightly buzzed.

"Come in," he grumbled, shoving the glass and bottle back under the desk.

Gabe poked his head inside, just as Jeremy predicted.

"Do you have a minute to review some of the pack financials? Neil's numbers just aren't making much sense." Pack betas traditionally handled pack finances, but it wouldn't surprise Jeremy one bit if Neil had shirked some of those responsibilities. It seemed like everywhere he looked, there was proof of his former beta cutting corners.

Gabe didn't wait for an answer, letting himself in and having a seat on the other side of the desk. Jeremy sighed, running his hands through his hair.

"Listen, Gabe...I appreciate your thoroughness, but honestly, this isn't a great time."

"Oh," he said, eyes lowering to the report. "Yeah, I can, uh, smell the liquor."

Jeremy scowled. "It's been a long day."

"Sure. I guess this can wait until tomorrow," Gabe said, setting the files down. "Okay, you've got my attention. What's up?"

Jeremy's eyebrows raised. "What do you mean?"

"I mean, what's up with you? I'm your beta, and you've been distracted, drunk, or both since I got here. What's causing you to go on a bender? Or is this just normal behavior for you?" Gabe held the alpha's gaze, almost challenging him to deny the truth. It was the sort of thing a seasoned second-in-command would do. For a naturally non-confrontational omega, he was settling into the beta position a little too well.

"It's nothing," Jeremy huffed. "I'm just not sleeping well, and all that shit with Neil is... well, shit. That's what it is."

"You're not sleeping well?" Gabe asked, frowning. "Do you have any other symptoms?"

"Symptoms? What are you a doctor now?" Jeremy glared at him, annoyed at being questioned. "Fine. Yeah, I've just been feeling... I don't know, a little restless, I guess. It doesn't matter. I'll be alright."

Gabe gave him a thoughtful look before collecting the files.

"You know, Jeremy, it sounds sort of how I was feeling before I met Ella for the first time. They say that sometimes males can sense when they're about to meet their true mate for the first time. Who knows? Maybe we'll have an alpha female soon."

"Get out of my office, Gabe." The last thing he needed was a mate to make a bad situation even worse. His wolf could grumble all he wanted, but Jeremy wasn't in any shape to take on a female. He was fine being on his own and was more than willing to set anyone straight who thought otherwise.

Author's Note

I fell in love with Gabe while writing *Tracking His True Mate,* and I have enjoyed seeing him grow as he pursued a relationship with Ella. They both deserve all the happiness in the world. Rest assured there will be more of their story incorporated in other books in this series.

I have much more planned for other paranormal romances, as well as additional stories that incorporate elements of BDSM and power exchange. Please follow me on Amazon, Facebook, or Fetlife if you are interested in updates.

Thank you for your feedback! Your reviews mean so much.

About the Author

LYNNE STEWART is a prolific reader and a lover of all things paranormal and interesting. During the day, she works as a librarian and likes spending time with her husband, their children, and pets. By night, she enjoys creating steamy romances with a little bite in them.